TICKET
TO
RIDE

TICKET
TO
RIDE

DENNIS POTTER

Vintage Books
A Division of Random House, Inc.
New York

FIRST VINTAGE BOOKS EDITION, SEPTEMBER 1989

Library of Congress Cataloging-in-Publication Data
Potter, Dennis.
    Ticket to ride/Dennis Potter.—1st Vintage Books ed.
        p. cm.
    ISBN 0-679-72353-6: $6.95
    I. Title.
  [PR6066.077T5 1989]
  823'.914—dc20   89-40152
                                                                           CIP

Manufactured in the United States of America
10 9 8 7 6 5 4 3 2 1

To Jane, my daughter. The first reader.

'And still, among it all, snatches of lovely oblivion, and
     snatches of renewal
odd, wintry flowers upon the withered stem, yet new
     strange flowers
such as my life has not brought forth before, new
     blossoms of me.'

D.H. LAWRENCE
from his poem 'Shadows'

1

A minute away from disaster, as he was thinking that nothing was the same any more, and that nothing could ever again be as sweet as it used to be, the tall and sharp-boned traveller in the corner seat let out the sigh of his body's premonition, shifted awkwardly as though his limbs were hurting him, and stared out through the dining-car window. A darkening stretch of September land was passing by, in a hurry.

His eyes looked for purchase, or a fixed object, but glazed before they found it. His head kept trying to tell him something, but he could not hear. At last, though, in exasperation at neglect, a thought lettered itself with determined precision, right in front of him, and exactly as though enclosed between upturned commas.

'Express trains do not go clackety-clackety-clack any more, nor are they so much a part of the countryside through which they travel.'

But why did this seem to be so important a revelation? And why did it feel so drenched in melancholy, much sadder than the dusk?

'The windows,' said his brain, in the same pedagogic tones, 'have a double skin, and are shaped like a screen. They are separating you from the land and the air. They cannot be opened.'

Damp fields were sliding by, indifferent, and a distant horse cropping grass did not bother to lift its head. It had the sky falling slowly down on to its back, and work enough to do.

The man staring through the glass had the momentary

illusion that everything out there beyond the double layer of glass, subdued by a gradually congealing gloom, belonged to a different time and another order, and one which was going to replace all that he knew and had once loved. There was undoubted threat in the stoop of the hedgerow, the cold aloofness of the single dead elm, and the narrowing, watchful sky pretending to die in its own light.

Oh, save us. Oh, protect me. Oh –

He switched his gaze from the train window with the abruptness of a man trying to deflect an unexpected grief.

At that moment, precisely on the turn, he lost all connection with his previous self. It was as swift a disaster as falling into an uncovered well, and breaking every bone in his body at the bottom of the shaft.

His mind, it was, that lay there in pieces; but he did not call out, nor make any lesser sign of distress.

Indeed, these first few seconds of otherness were suddenly shimmering with a glancing, silvery light, touching things and then skeetering off them. He felt a tremble of freedom, matching the quick dance of the light. He did not yet know what had happened to him.

Three middle-aged businessmen who shared his table in the crowded restaurant compartment were putting forks to their mouths and sipping at their wineglasses. In these first moments, the utensils gleamed and flashed, and the liquid in the translucent petals glowed in all manner of amber and fire. He could watch them, in and through the shimmer, with wonder and with affection. Perhaps even with amusement.

Wayward light removed itself, but the oddities remained. Eating. Drinking. Moving the pouches of their cheeks like that. And look at the prongs on the fork! What strange objects. What funny things to do.

He felt himself shrinking back into his own space, and looked down to see what awaited him. He was surprised to find a partly eaten fish there.

6

Half a pound of tuppenny rice
Half a pound of treacle

The tune was definitely inside him, but where had it come from? Who were these people? What was this fish? Why was there so much movement? What am I doing here?

I? Who is I?

The windows have a double skin, and are shaped like a screen. They are separating you from the land and the air. They cannot be . . .

Opened-opened-opened rocked and bumped in the suddenly cavernous and echoing space between the bones of his skull. One sentence, it seemed, was all that it knew it had known, one description, ending on a word that would not stop.

The panic came up the lining of his throat in a yellow nausea, hit the back of his clenching teeth, and fell back again to leave a mouth that was almost too dry to make words with, too foul to accommodate their possible sense.

'Excuse me,' he tried to say, and made a noise.

They looked at him.

'Excuse me,' he struggled again, producing less of a croak. A face frowned at him.

But it still seemed to be too dificult to get the spikes of the harder sounds free of his lips and gums and tongue, which were locked together in a dry paste made of filth.

He gave up, and stared down at the remnants of the fish on the plate in front of him. A ridge of bone cried out to him, and he shut it off. The mutilated wedge of lemon then as violently demanded his attention, smarting at its wounds, swallowing an acid pride to call for help. Its citrine glare pointed towards a *cipollino* puddle of lumpy sauce. He saw, now, that in front of him was an old and blighted plateau, where strange creatures screamed and sobbed as they coiled themselves into the tormented postures of a totally alien agony.

'The love of our Lord Jesus Christ,' came up at him, in what seemed to be a voice he ought to know. It was important to sit still, to sit very still . . .

' – and I said to him,' the man on his right was saying, as his head cleared, 'I said to him, if you are telling me you use earnings per share as your one and only yardstick –' heavy spectacles, heavy lips, thick grey sideburns, all in the same motion of irritation ' – I said, then you have placed yourself at the mercy of easily manipulated quantities – '

'That's absolutely right,' said the much fatter man opposite, but in a slightly bored way, content to use agreement as a punctuation rather than a support.

'*Excuse me –* '

Oh, it is no more than a dry rasp, a mere whisper. But I know I want to speak. I can understand what is being said. I am not mad –

No, said the fish. Yes, shrieked the lemon. Don't care, don't care, said a chip as thick as a severed thumb, basking with greasy insolence in a previously unnoticed canyon between the two.

He tried to ignore everything but the men who were talking at each other. The plate of unfinished food was sabotaging him.

'They call it creative accounting, I believe,' the third man was saying. But his eyes were distracted, excited perhaps, and flickering elsewhere. At me. At Me! He is aware that I am trying to speak. He might even be my friend. My colleague.

'Earnings per share is the thing that attracts the punter, you see, and although there are better measures of – '

'Excuse me – ?'

They looked at him. The words had definitely been spoken. And once he knew this, the hardening paste in his throat and in his mouth suddenly came free. A form of grace had returned: and with it, embarrassment.

'I do beg your pardon,' he said, aware now that he must have been a well-mannered man, and conscious that anything he said was going to be inappropriate, or worse. 'I'm sorry to intrude. I know this will seem rather strange, but – '

He stopped. It was too absurd to continue.

'Yes?'

The inevitable prompt came from the fat man of the three. The set of his face showed that there could be no escape into silence. It was no good running away with your eyes into the fields on the other side of the window. There was no sanctuary in the strangely articulate plate of food, nor in the gently juddering glass of wine. *Tink-tink!* it was saying, the start of some kind of message. The alignment of the knives, the forks and the spoons on the white cloth was full of significance, he realized. It was foolish to talk to those who might be his enemies – and probably were – until he had deciphered these messages and signals.

'What is it? What's wrong?' said one of the three.

He looked up at the man who had spoken, for the voice was not, after all, a hostile one. He let himself release the imbecility he already knew his question to be.

'Can you please tell me – I mean. Forgive me. But am I by any chance *with* you? We are not travelling together, are we?'

In the terror of the small silence which followed, he heard the thought in his head again which told him that the window separated him from the land and from the air, and could not be opened.

'On the same train, do you mean?'

It was the man on his right who said it, but all three of them started to laugh.

But then something stopped them. Their faces changed.

'What is it?' came the fat man's voice, and he could hear the concern in it, clear through the slop and splash and whisper of everything else. 'What is the matter – ?'

9

Oh, don't let me cry. Please do not allow me to cry.

They had all stopped lifting their forks to their mouths. They were not pouching out their cheeks. They were not moving their eyes.

He knew that he could not hold the pitch of their attention. They would absorb him into their own flesh. He dropped his eyes, needing refuge. But then he saw that one of the soiled plates on the table before him had crept slyly across the cloth, carrying its crumbled burden towards the stem of the nearest wineglass.

As the more opaque china touched, nudged and then nudged again the lighter and translucent material, it showed resentment at its own stolidity, and began to chide the glass with a rapid, growing *chink-chink* of reproval. The sound reached into him, and he shared in the moral accusation, wise enough to know that the confrontation had nothing to do with the vibration of the train as it plunged headlong into the still thickening dusk.

He suspected that not everyone knew the extent to which things spoke to each other, and argued amongst themselves. But the *chink-chink-chink* was becoming the most urgent sound in the whole of this murmuring creation. It began to irritate.

This is not right, he thought. This cannot be. Someone must break into this dream. Help me.

He looked up, and saw their eyes on him. It was vital that he tried to make them understand. Plop! like a stone in a pond, he saw what he had been seeing when this new state began. He tried to control his voice.

'I was looking out of the window here – ' rap-rap on the glass 'at a horse which was cropping the gr– '

Chink-chink-chink-chink.

The word broke in two on the edge of his teeth, but they were still staring, their faces immobile.

'Please,' he said, 'just a moment.'

He pushed the plate away from the glass, hoping that they would not notice. The tips of his fingers prickled oddly as he touched the china. A word flew straight at him from his unknown past. *Scabious*. Field scabious.

A flat, round flower-head, coloured like the lilac, high above the dull green leaves. The juice of the wild flower, that was what had sent the word. Or is it memory that prickles and stings?

What has this to do with me?

More haunting than the meadow bloom was the flash he had had of the tip of a sharp pencil, forming the letters.

Why? Where? What for?

'You were looking out of the window – ,' prompted the fat man.

He nodded, and nodded again, on his own swallow, leaving the problem of field scabious for some other time.

'At a horse,' he said.

The plate was wilfully edging towards the wineglass once more. He could feel his skin prickle and sting. Why had he mentioned the horse? The animal had not looked up. It didn't care. But these, the people, were still fixing on him. He had to try again, if only to switch off their eyes.

'And when I turned my head away,' he said, desperately hoping that the plate would not again nudge the glass, 'I – just a moment!'

He pushed the plate away violently, and some of the stuff on it went wet against his thumb.

'I realized,' he continued, 'that I did not know where I was, or where I was going, or where I had been, or – who I am. I don't know who I am.'

He could see that they did not know what to say. In their confusion, he surreptitiously wiped the filth off his thumb at the bottom edge of the cloth.

'It wasn't the horse – ' he tried to say, but was unable to get it out. The tears had sprung to his eyes with such force that they splashed out on to his face before he could get a hand up. The noise of crying preceded his recognition of it as his own. He sobbed. He could not stop. A dry, retching-like sound. His hands scrabbled out in front of him, and he had great difficulty in getting them up to his unknown and disintegrating face.

'Oh, I say – dear, dear – '

'Now, now, old chap! Now, now – '

'Hey, hold on. Hold on.'

There wasn't much they could say, or do. Everyone else in the dining car had by now also stopped eating, drinking and talking. A knife clattered hard down at the next table, and further along towards the rushing engine a spindly old woman with a cardigan and a Fabian air was standing up in her place in order to see more clearly the cause of the commotion. Indignation, concern, helplessness: very Fabian.

A uniformed steward came at a near trot down the aisle, with the roll of a sailor and a peculiar sort of pleasure on his face.

'Anything wrong here, gents?' he asked, practically out of breath. 'Is everything all right?'

The redundancy of the question was made more comical by the relish of its delivery. The two things together were better at checking the sobs than a more sympathetic query delivered in less obvious zest.

'Everything – ' the weeper gasped, swallowing sobs, and pounding hard enough on his chest to bruise the bone, 'everything is – coming up roses.'

The fat man snickered, then controlled himself.

'Well, I hope it's nothing that has been caused by the food, sir,' said the steward.

'For God's sake!' hissed one of the other three at the table, while someone else further along sat on an embarrassed hilarity.

'It's my job, sir,' said the steward, offended.

'But can't you see this man is not well – !'

'I can see that very well, sir, and it's my job to make sure there's nothing amiss with – what was it the gentleman had? The fish. Yes.'

'God almighty,' whispered the fat man, rolling up his eyes.

'I have lost my memory,' said the object of all their concern, in a newly decisive voice. He was sure now of the nature of his plight.

'You've what, sir?' asked the steward.

'I do not know who I am. I do not know what I am doing here, apart from embarrassing myself and, it seems, everyone else. It was a shock, and I felt very upset, but I understand what has happened now. I'm sorry about all the fuss.'

He could hear that his speech was measured and shaped in a formal way, and that it was decisive and even authoritative. I feel – he thought – that I can see the curl of the comma up ahead, and the boulder of the full stop. I wonder what I am.

'In the circumstances,' he was continuing, 'it might be advisable for me to have a hot drink. Perhaps you would be kind enough to bring me some coffee?'

'Certainly, sir.'

'Oh, and to take my plate away.'

'At once, sir.' The steward might have been talking to simply another well-bred passenger. He spun around at once, almost stamped his feet, and went away up the rocking aisle, with a sailor's walk but a soldier's stupidity.

The three businessmen stared at the amnesiac. The manner in which he had regained control of himself had saved them from embarrassment but only at the cost of uneasy suspicion and obscure resentment.

'What to do? What to do?' the man said, with the hint of a chuckle.

'Look in your wallet,' the fat man said.

'I beg your pardon?'

'Turn out your pockets!'

13

'Oh. Yes. Yes, of course. Thank you very much.'

He spoke politely, but he resented what seemed to be a command. And what would be in his jacket? Is there some danger here?

Groping inside his clothes, with anxiety, he registered that the silvery-grey cloth was of good quality, soberly cut, and a little worn. Be careful, a voice seemed to say, his and yet not his, be very careful.

'You know me. You trust me,' said this other voice, him and not him. He strained inside himself to listen, but it fell silent.

They watched him too closely as he opened his wallet, and he did not like it. Attend, he thought, to your own affairs.

The wallet, too, was of the best kind, with a fat and crinkly near-squeak to the touch. He hoped it had not been made out of the skin unrolled from the back of a slaughtered pig. An image of something unimaginably hideous almost formed, but was incapable of holding shape, and retreated in the faintest haze of blood.

Oh, what is it I have done? What terrible thing?

'It's not your fault,' said the other voice, already familiar, deep inside him, and yet not a part of him.

They watched his fingers pull out a thick wad of crisp new banknotes. The greeny brown murmur of fifty-pound notes. His own and the other three's expressions changed at the sight of them. There must be three or four thousand pounds here.

One of the businessmen made a sound like a whistle being forced into a cough.

'Credit cards,' someone else said.

'This money – ' he gasped, feeling the dampness of newly released sweat beneath his shirt. 'All this money – '

'That's a lot to be carrying around.'

'Credit cards. They'll have your name on them.'

'Driving licence. Anything like that.'

What have I done? Oh, what have I done?

'Membership card or something – ?

'You should be careful. All that cash on you – '

'No credit cards?'

'What about a driving licence?'

He wanted them to shut up now. There was nothing at all they could do for him. Their embarrassment and their concern had been displaced by their curiosity. Why was it so difficult for people to mind their own business? *I know this type. I know them.* The kind who would snuffle and grunt about in the smallest tuck and fold of your life, if you gave them half a chance. He saw, and scorned, the moistening of their lips and the darting eagerness in their eyes. The tell-tale marks of the human predator.

Solitary. Solitary. Let me be solitary. Leave me alone!

There were no credit cards in his wallet, which the three observers thought was strange, or perhaps vaguely immoral. There was no driving licence. His name, whatever it was, was not written upon anything in his pockets. Perhaps, as one of them pointed out, there would be an identifiable label from a local tailor in his suit, but he was certainly not going to divest himself of his jacket here and now, in front of these eager eyes.

'Most people, you know, carry some sort of clue to their identity,' the man on his right was saying, with a trace of indignation he obviously did not keep for the earnings-per-share measurement alone.

'Can you really remember *nothing*? Get hold of any one recollection, and follow the thread of it . . .'

'You were already on the train when we got on. That was at Swindon.'

'So you must have travelled from Bristol Parkway, Newport, Cardiff or one of those other places in Wales.'

'You don't sound Welsh. I'll bet that's a relief, eh?'

'What does your ticket say – oh. No. The tickets have been

15

collected. You haven't got a ticket, have you? The tickets which expire at Paddington have been collected.'

'You haven't got a return from wherever it was you started from.'

'Unless he started from London.'

Leave me alone. Stop it. Be quiet.

'Yes. Unless you came *from* London, and are returning there.'

London? The word stung, and he became aware of his genitals. London Bridge is burning down, my fair lady.

'Or unless you had a single ticket.'

Leave me alone!

'Of course, I suppose you have no recollection of where you're supposed to be going when you get to the station. God, that would scare me.'

'You didn't seem to have any keys on you. Do you have any keys? I said – do you have any keys?'

A cup of coffee had appeared in front of him. When did it come? He watched a thin wisp of steam curl on the top of it and float away. That's me, he thought. Me.

'The best thing you could do – well, I don't know actually. I don't know what to advise you, but – '

Nothing, tell me nothing. Stop talking. Let me go.

'Best thing he could do would be to talk to the police. Go to a police station as soon as you arrive at Paddington.'

Faces, faces, opening and stretching, eyes narrowing and widening, teeth showing every now and again behind the soft mollusc of the boggy lip. Noses packed with hair and slime. Bumps and ridges and pocks and brown moles, leering down in a sweaty lather as their bodies emptied into – into – my fair lady . . .

Police? Who said police?

His nerves jumped, all together. He lifted up his cup, to try to hide a part, at least, of his face.

'They're supposed to be the professionals, after all. They must have some idea of what to do.'

'Mind you. I wouldn't bank on it. Not with the kind of people they get nowadays.'

Police? No, not the police. Stay well clear.

He could see the reflection darkly wavering of what must be his own face in the hot coffee, and he tilted the cup away quickly, spilling a little.

The others had fallen silent at last. The predatory excitement went out of their eyes. His silence, his indifference, had made them return their attentions to their plates. They did not know what else to do, now that he himself refused to be eaten.

2

What can I do? Where can I go? Where can I stay?

Each question advanced, receded, then swept towards him again, in a vertiginous whirl, laden with city dust and human smells.

He stood earthbound in the jostling evening crowds at Paddington Station, with no luggage, no name, and no past. Everything was as though it had not been defined. He pondered a little on the nature of freedom, and in doing so recognized himself as a serious man. Good. By small means, and perhaps the discovery of this or that habit, he might be able to tip one impression into another and so begin a cascade which would deliver him back to himself.

'No. You don't want that,' said the voice which had spoken to him, or from him, while sitting in the train. He looked around to see who it was who had addressed himself so intimately, and then stopped, sensing that this was not the right thing to do.

He allowed his eyes to wander. There were people everywhere. But none of them was as free as he was. They each had a label to attend to, a call to obey. I am not attached. I can soar to whatever state or condition I wish to create for myself . . .

The light in which he might have flown had been sucked out of the air beyond the great, vaulted roof. He could not taste his freedom, not here, not like this. The artificial and sourly orange glow that had replaced the day seemed now to be squeezing out into the space around him from the linings of his own scraped and emptied mind.

What can I do? Where can I go? Where can I stay?

A loudspeaker was spilling out a booming garble of place names. One of these, perhaps, contained the dwelling which a few hours earlier he had known as 'home'.

Home. The word went plop! Again, it was like a stone or a pebble being tossed into a pond. But no picture came. There were no ripples.

Home. A house. Who else lived there? A house. A stairs. A bed. Who else lived there?

His eyes seemed to pick out, with their own will, a young woman more attractive than the rest, with long hair and little black boots, moving with a slight sway through the packs of people.

> Half a pound of tuppenny rice
> Half a pound of treacle

The little nursery rhyme irritated him, and he wondered why it had got off the train with him.

What to do? Where to go?

It was too late to find a doctor, or, at least, too late to find a good one. The same warning jabs as before told him not to seek out a police station. Not yet. Not tonight. Perhaps, not ever.

But what have I done? Do I have any reason to fear the law? Perhaps his emptied brain was the sign that some previous act had set him apart from the human community.

Not a single one of his doubts or questions which nipped and snarled at the back of his eyes was capable of being answered. The subdued ache at the back of his eyes was threatening to become more assertive. He put a thumb and forefinger to the bridge of his nose, and pressed.

A sharp-edged suitcase carried by someone in a hurry banged against the back of his legs. There was no apology.

People. The thing to do, the one certain course of action, surely, was to get away from people. He cast his eyes around and about to look at them, and felt sick. The station forecourt was a gaseous swamp in which noisy and ungainly bipeds moved with difficulty, baying and grunting, stickied and unclean. How do such shambling creatures reproduce themselves? Sticks of bone and sinew poking into hairy holes.

He did not want to be touched by any one of them. He did not even want their dull, dead eyes to rest upon him. Oh, to flee! Oh, to ascend beyond the clammy reach of such a herd!

He began to walk across the station forecourt, often switching his body sideways to avoid the thrust of other shoulders, and what he knew would be the beast-like stench of another's breath. He became aware, with relief, that his feet knew better than he what to do. They seemed to recognize this place from the lost times. He was being borne away on good stout shoes, which were properly polished, he was glad to see.

And when he saw the blue and gold canopy above the heavy glass-pannelled doors to the back entrance of the big old Victorian hotel which fronted the station, it seemed almost as though he had been looking for it.

The mysterious and abandoned past might itself steal back towards him by such small movements. If that was what he wanted, he could be led across the shards and fragments towards a real, a whole, piece of memory.

'But I don't even know what day of the week it is.'

'Sorry?' said a man at his side, looking at him.

He mumbled a dismissal, and veered off quickly, in a fluster of alarm. This was bad. Evidently, he was now talking to himself. The boundary between In and Out must have changed. He tightened his lips against each other to make sure that they could not release anything, and pushed hard at the doors to the hotel.

Behind him, in the turmoil he was escaping, the station announcer had resumed his over-resonant boom. In this further list of buttery English place names, stretching down into Cornwall, one especial word clarified itself in the amplified gabble.

' – ' and Estrangement,' said the receding loudspeaker, before the voice dropped back once again into the nearly incomprehensible, the harder consonants reflected back in the shallow puddles of their own echoes. *'Ich habe mich verirrt,'* it seemed to say, which made no sense.

' – ' and Estrangement,' the list continued, second time around, as the heavy doors swung back into place behind him.

'Oh, surely not,' he said to himself, keeping his lips safely tight together. 'There can be no such place. The inhabitants would not accept it.'

A banistered column of stone steps tilted towards him, but his feet knew what to do, and his hand reached for the metal support without hesitation.

'Surely not,' he said again. 'Not "Estrangement". Anyone would think that it was in the county of Alienation.'

He began to smile as he ascended, his shoes ringing bravely on the stone. It was possible that there was more wit in the world than he had been prepared to acknowledge, standing out there in the milling crowds. Why shouldn't there be a place called Estrangement, with its own railway station, fast-food bars and funeral parlours?

Half a pound of tuppenny rice . . .

Yes. Why not such a town? He would adapt it with a small shift of letters into his address on the registration card, and shuffle another gene or so to sign himself in as John Buck rather than the law-book John Doe.

. . . Half a pound of treacle . . .

'Find a burrow,' he said to himself, alone. And dig in.

3

A dream took too long to sink back into the impregnable hinterlands of its proper realm. A slender young woman in black ankle boots was still tossing shiny little pieces of a polished black stone into a pond of black water, a pensive infant beside her with a blank face but a flop of silky black ribbon in her hair. A bird flew down with wide wings and picked up one of the falling stones in its beak and flapped away again.

He could see them clearly, even as his waking eyes began to take in the brighter patterns at the tall window, with wooden toggles, on the other side of his room.

First the lovely young woman and then the featureless child, each too late, called across to the line of reeds on the opposite bank, in clear and high voices, not shrill, which nevertheless could not be understood. It was a name. She must be calling the name, the woman. And it could only be his name.

Who am I?

He strained to hear her, and tried to get back into the fast-retreating dream, but already the wall opposite him in the hotel room and the reeds on the other side of the water had become the same substance. The woman and the incomplete child were no more. They had receded into the unfinished explanation, stealing away with his name.

Who? *Who?* rose up in vain through the last splash of stone in the black water and the first fold of the curtain at the hotel window, before standing naked in front of him with no sleep in its eyes.

John Buck, self-named, jerked suddenly up in the bed and swung his feet to the floor, so that they landed beside his own shoes. They startled him. It was almost as though there were someone standing in the shoes, familiar and yet unknown, real but not there. He felt his mind teeter away and then tilt back into himself, and sensed that one part of it was eager to interrogate the other.

'Who are you?' he said, hearing the words come out from between his teeth in a hiss. Which one was he talking to?

He sat completely still, for minutes on end, trying to be one again. When he had succeeded, he remained as still as before, and worked his will as hard as before, in an attempt to dredge up a whole piece of memory. But his past stayed in the deeps, beyond light, out of reach.

The dream was the only clue, except for the name of the wild flower which had come to him in a tingle of his skin on the train. But the dream had someone else in it, and a word calling out to him. He concentrated on the dream.

Nothing else was added to it. He scraped and scraped at it, but it would yield no more than the black water, the swooping bird, the figures of woman and child, and the overwhelming melancholy.

No. The furthest back into his past that he could go was the sight through a screen-shaped, double-skinned and unopenable window of a horse cropping grass half an acre of fading light away from a single dead elm.

'Horse?' he said, standing up. 'Fuck the horse!'

The sudden vigour of the word and movement also gave him the realization that he was fully clothed.

Strange! He was sure that he had put his bare feet to the floor, beside his untenanted shoes. He thought he had seen tiny tufts of carpet settling around his toes. But this could not have been so. He was dressed.

Reflecting upon it, he decided that he must have fallen into a deep sleep as soon as he had thrown himself upon the bed, which had been immediately after the front door had clicked shut upon an unnecessary porter who had been surprised by the generosity of the tip.

Three minutes past ten o'clock. Bright light flooding the window, and the noise of the morning traffic. So he had slept for more than thirteen hours. Four or five seconds of the sleep had provided the remnant of the dream. What other melancholy images were working within him for all the other minutes?

He stared at his watch. A police car ooh-aahed in the street down below, and he frowned at the sound, but did not look up.

He kept staring at the watch. Tick-tick-tick-tick. A quartz tick, which has no tock. Tick-tick-tick. The small sound, growing in response to his attention, demanded something of him. Tick-tick-tick – urgent, urgent, urgent – and he knew what it was: a matter of life and death that he find out at-once-at-once-at-once who he was and where he belonged.

Twelve minutes past eleven. Eleven? But he had not seen the move of the little hand. A whole hour must have been used up by his former, or his other, self.

In a hurry now, sucking in his breath, he swiftly unbuckled the watch, and turned it over and over in his hands, not sure what he was looking for. It was made of gold, and was as thin as a wafer. The second hand revolved in abrupt little starts. There was no scratch, no inscription, no sign of particular ownership.

'Most people, you know, carry some sort of clue to their identity,' a peevish voice on the train had said. If that were true, then it was a question of his own diligence in hunting down the clue.

He took off all his clothes.

Slowly and carefully, determined not to miss a thing, he went through them, inch by inch, poring over every crease and fold, every button, every tag and label, fingers delving, nose sniffing.

The handkerchief was white and starchy, without initials or design. His tie was neither striped nor institutional. He did not have a cheque book or a pen or a railway ticket or a pocket comb or even a single unattached hair. There were no odd smells, no minuscule stains. Indeed, he could as well have fallen to earth from another planet, newly kitted by whoever had sent him.

A service trolley squeaked on its castors in the passage outside his room. He cocked his head, for the sound appeared to be on the point of yielding up something else. It meant something.

Looking through the fish-eye peep-hole in his door, he surveyed what he could see of the corridor. A room-service waiter passed from view. He heard the knuckle-rap on another door, and the soft call, 'Room service.'

And then he saw himself at a door like this, his eye to the peep-hole, his forehead against the wood, looking out on to another corridor. A beautiful woman was outside the door. She had just tap-tapped, and was in the act of standing back, a smile fixed, her chin tilted a little. She looked like a girl about to hum a catchy tune. Then she shifted, made as if to look at her watch, stopped herself, and the crook of her long fingers came up towards the door in order to knock again.

But the insight or the memory or whatever it was dropped away suddenly, before her fingers reached the wood.

He looked out now on an empty and a different corridor, the present one, or the real one, and no effort would place her back in position. He looked down at his still unclothed body. His penis had reared up hard and expectant into his hand.

'But she's a whore,' he said, in a whisper.

Grief swept through him, and his penis went slack again. He looked at the pile of his clothes on the bed, and shook his head slowly from side to side in dumb misery.

That woman, whoever she was, must also be the woman

throwing polished stones into the pond. If he could find her, she would perhaps tell him who he was.

'But she's dead,' he said, out loud.

The sound of his voice saying this was immediately loathsome to him. He told himself that he was picking up nothing but the random and the accidental, and that there was no method with his present knowledge of distinguishing between reality and imagination, fantasy and dream. Until and unless he discovered who he was, everything was without meaning.

He could get nothing out of his clothes. But what about his shoes? Look at the way they are beckoning to me!

He peered like a detective at the almost completely unworn soles, and sniffed at their leathery newness. Why did everything he wore appear to have been bought the day before yesterday? Was this in itself a clue? Did not criminals and murderers burn or otherwise dispose of all their clothes after they . . . ?

No. No. Stop it.

He had nowhere else to look, but, in case, he pushed his fingers through his hair, rubbed his tongue against the back of his teeth, examined his fingernails, and looked between his toes. He flexed each arm, and then each leg. Nothing.

There could not be any doubt. His former self had deliberately and efficiently removed every single trace of personal identity. Moreover, this must surely have been done before the amnesia. But could one anticipate the loss of memory? Was it possible to plan it, or induce it? Are there drugs which can do that?

He pushed away the speculation. Chance was less threatening than design. 'That is why atheism is attractive,' prickled his mind. Accident was more reassuring than intention.

Still naked, he went to examine himself in the bathroom mirror, which hummed and twitched with light. A ventilator

26

turned itself on at the same time. White tiles shone coldly, and he knew that if he spoke there would be a ceramic echo.

He was surprised by the baleful hostility in the violet eyes which stared back at him from the full-length mirror. And then by the unfamiliarity of the face in which they were set. He put a hand up to touch his cheek, and saw his reflection do the same. 'That is me,' he thought, and then said it out loud, in case it would make the discovery any less true.

The body was better by far than he had expected it to be. It strained and quivered with energy, as though held back by a leash. Or was it only that he was trembling?

The mirror showed him a man in his early or possibly middle thirties. Tall, fair-skinned, with no tanning. The hands, as he already knew, showed no signs of hard labour.

'He looks ready to spring,' he said to his own image, which did indeed stand on the balls of the feet, not exactly leaning forward, but showing that it was ready to do so.

There were no welts or bruises on the tall and fine-downed body. No lumps or bumps or bites or boils. No needle holes. No damage. Teeth good. Gums in order. Tongue not coated or discoloured. He was a fit man, on the outside.

There is something you have to do.

He did not speak the words and it did not feel as though he had thought them. They came like an instruction, as from another voice, but with such clarity that he said, 'What?' and then saw that he was speaking to his own reflection only. He stared.

'John Buck,' he said, eventually, and watched the baleful expression drain out of his imperious blue eyes, making his face less like a blade.

'Hello, John Buck,' in some way assented the figure in the mirror, who yesterday afternoon had got on a train somewhere west of Swindon in the middle of England as another person, with a deeper life or a longer memory.

Another, whom he had murdered.

The thought did not come to the man and his reflection, newly made John Buck, that it might be better expressed the other way around.

4

'John – ' began Helen, deliberately brisk, as she opened the door of what they now called The Work Room, forgetting to knock before doing so, in a way that had now become frequent enough to show she must have resented the original injunction. He had so-say insisted upon it with one of his momentary frowns, about five months ago.

She was surprised not to find him stooped over the long bench.

The brisk entry had been because she had expected the quick, potentially resentful turn of what she thought of as his beautiful head. The would-be combative thrust that less and less often became as quickly transformed by his slow, rather sheepish smile, and the half-apologetic spread of his hand as he indicated the intricacies of his work.

Where was he?

One of the things which had at first irritated and now more seriously alarmed her about these last few months of their marriage was the total inflexibility of his new working routine. 'Discipline,' he called it, his mouth making a shape like a wince, as it seemed to her.

Four days a week from eight in the morning until six in the evening, and the Friday from seven until noon, he hunched over the severed heads or exposed roots of English wild flowers and weeds, the bench scattered with earth and bits of foliage, then turned to the white cards on the board, and back again to the bloom or leaf, stem, twig or bud. He had an automatic coffee-pot bubbling on a shelf, clicking at times to its thermostat, a packet of dry biscuits, and a plate of

Cheddar or Double Gloucester cheese cut into small and precise cubes – and that was all, for the entire span of the long working day. The monkish day.

No telephone. No booze. No idle staring into space. No conversation, radio, television, newspapers or magazines. No catching up on the cricket scores, as once was the case. And, officially, no other kinds of intrusion or interruption 'unless it is vital, by which I mean really necessary'.

'Like life or death?' she had laughed.

He had simply looked at her, without a smile, and nodded, 'Like life or death. Precisely,' and resumed his work.

The longest break into the working routine had come about five weeks ago, on a slow and heavy Thursday afternoon brooding towards a thunderstorm. Blackening clouds, not yet banked together, were hanging in the sky, exhausted. She had twitched her foot a few times, looked at the clock a few more times, chewed her lower lip, and, finally, wanting to ask so many questions under the one 'What is wrong?', had entered this green and slightly dank oblong of a room without either a tip-tap on the door or an explicitly vital reason.

'John – ' and he had jumped.

'I'm sorry, John, but – '

'You see what happens when you come in without warning!'

'I didn't mean to make you jump – '

'My hand jerks, that's what happens. I lose the line, and I am on the finest of silver hairs at this precise moment.'

'Oh, John. I'm sorry, I didn't mean – '

'Lady's mantle,' he said, without inflexion.

'What?'

His eyes had not moved as he examined her. She felt a tiny clutch of fear. There had been many men in the past who had scrutinized her in this way, but they had also been anonymous, and all but faceless. Physical intimacies held no threat for her: it was the personal which caused a flutter of nerves.

'Lady's mantle,' he repeated, eyes still on her. 'I am work-ing on one of the little plants to be found upon the unregarded wayside. A variety popularly known as lady's mantle – although that particular adverb is getting to be less and less appropriate as time goes by.'

There it was again. The odd formality and stiffness of his sentences. From the first day she had known him, his speech had always sounded to her as though he had written it down in advance, or was quoting, with a slight satiric edge, from some more self-important predecessor. But it had not been as bad as this, his way of talking. Something was going on. He was changing.

'John. I'm – I thought we ought to talk – '

'Do you know what they used to use it for? The country people of not so very long ago?'

She hesitated. His blue eyes were still too steadily upon her, but she thought there was a new light in them. Never, despite the nature of their beginnings with each other, not once had he looked at her with contempt. But now – *oh, don't*, she had cried inside, *don't look at me like this!* – now, he was staring just short of a sneer. She shook her head.

He put down one of his almost needle-fine brushes in a groove of an extremely neat tray, stood up with a scrape of his high stool, and advanced so implacably upon her that, for a moment, she had to put down an urge to step backwards.

'Tits,' he said.

'What?'

'Boobs.'

She tried a tentative smile, but his eyes had gone darker.

'It was thought to be a specific to firm up the sag of a woman's breast, this plant. An infusion of its flower-head was alleged to be a means of restoring their upthrust or bounce or, as I would once have preferred to think of it, their *lift*.'

Her smile, small and unsure as it was, met no reflection. She broadened it, though her heart was bumping.

'You think I need it, this what-did-you-call-it?' she asked, trusting to her natural lightness of tone.

'*Alchemilla vulgaris*,' he said, 'Lady's mantle.'

'Oh,' she said. What else? 'Ah' was also possible.

'No. I do not think you do. It would serve no purpose whatsoever in your case.'

Smile, she thought, why don't you smile?

'Well, thank goodness for that,' she laughed.

He reached out, and placed his hand over her right breast. It seemed to her as though he had done it with the same kind of meticulous precision as the way he was now speaking. His violet eyes had not flickered. They did not stray from her face.

'I like that,' she lied.

'Do you now? Do you really? Well, well. Fancy that.'

'John – ?'

His fingers, stiffer than they usually were, and far from gentle, as he mostly always was, pulled at the silky stuff of her top until they released her breast. Unknowingly, she braced her legs. Knowingly, she smiled.

'When I first saw this,' he said, dropping his eyes at last to her exposed breast, 'I could not help but wonder how it had preserved such a pure and innocent look – '

'No,' she said. 'No, John. No. Don't.'

'It seemed miraculous to me that not one of the men who had enjoyed themselves here had spoilt it by biting off the nipple.'

Her throat had closed up.

Suddenly, he was rolling her nipple between his teeth, carefully, but still not gently enough.

She made herself look straight ahead to the copper and glass terrarium, filled with what she thought was a sort of bell heather, busy and pink, but indisputably near to death.

'Ow!' she wanted to say but didn't.

Was this it, then? Was the impossible past obtruding itself at last, and the delayed punishment already here?

'Petal,' he seemed to say, his mouth occupied.

She coiled her fingers into the tuftier hair at the back of his head, and tilted back a little. But he pulled his mouth away, and she saw, with a swift dance of pain, that his eyes were full of tears.

'Next,' he said, 'I do the orpine. The woodland's flush.'

'John?'

He shook his head with an awful, slow deliberation.

'That's if I'm allowed to get on without interruption.'

'Come out of here!' she yelled. 'Come out of this room! Come on! Now!'

'Come out?' he looked at her, suddenly bewildered. 'Oh, but I can't do that!'

'What do you mean you can't?' she said, surprised at the force of her words. 'Of course you fucking well can!'

'Helen,' he said, more severely than his wet eyes ought to have allowed, 'there's no longer any need for you to talk like a whore. I'd appreciate it if you did not do so to *me*, at least.'

He then placed her exposed breast back behind the silk, looked hard at her and turned away.

Leaving me for dead, she thought.

'John. Oh, John,' she said, in distress. 'What has happened? What has brought all this up? Why won't you talk to me about it? Why are you trying to hide yourself away in here?'

He turned his face back towards her. She was astonished to see that his mouth appeared to be about to twist out of his own control, and that his expression, and all of him, had a completely uncharacteristic tremble or quiver.

But as she moved towards him, he brought his face back into his own ownership, and lifted his hand.

'I am not hiding,' he said. 'I am working. I will stop working at the time laid down to stop. I am trying to

33

discipline myself, and I suggest you try to do the same. I have to try to live down my indolence, and you, your shame.'

He turned abruptly away from her, in his own blaze, but before he got back to his bench, and the fine silvery hairs beneath the lobes of the lady's mantle, he stopped, as suddenly as a riven creature, and stared at the tiled floor.

'I beg your pardon,' he said, not lifting his eyes.

She took her chance by asking, in a voice as quiet as his had just been, why they could not talk about what was so obviously troubling him. They had promised each other that 'the past' was an irrelevance between them. She had not spoken of it, except by accident, so why had he?

But he had continued to stare down at the tiles, and she had realized that he was not even listening to her.

'What's so special about the fucking tiles?' she had cried at the last. A big mistake.

For one moment she thought he was going to hit her, but instead he had gone on back to the bench.

He picked up his brush, and dipped it, and began to work colour into the white card on his drawing board, leaving her stranded. She became aware of a clove-like smell from some wild herb or other, injured in an open box in the far corner, which hinted at the rank and the spiritually unclean.

This had taken place on a Thursday afternoon, five weeks ago. The sky had cleared itself with the drama of a thunderstorm, but the pair of them had not gone on to a similar resolution.

It was the worst moment of their short marriage.

Worse, even, than that day in the spring of the year when he had driven the muddied Range Rover the hundred or so miles back from the Charlotte Street area of London, in the middle of the afternoon, to announce that he had resigned his art director's job at the advertising agency – and then, hating the lie more than the humiliation, that he had been booted out.

34

'Let go,' he spat out, suddenly. 'They say let go. They can't bring themselves to say sacked or fired. They speak American. They think they *are* American. They tell me I've been Let Go.'

'What's that on your shirt?' she had asked, stupidly, but disorientated by what was then, for him, an unusual venom.

He had turned a violet stare upon her.

'Curry,' he said, as though addressing a slow child. 'I dropped some of my lunch. The fork slipped. Or my mouth went loose. I leave you to work out which.'

'It doesn't matter – ' she began, not sure whether she was speaking of the shirt, the job, the fork, his mouth, her question, or his new manner and his violet stare.

'*Taka Del*, or *Del Taka*,' he said. 'An inherently sloppy accompaniment to what is already sufficiently moist.'

And then he had frowned, hearing his own strange construction. She thought at first that he had spoken like this in some sort of mimicry, perhaps of a colleague, or the man who had sacked him. But, no. In the couple of hours driving the car home, he had changed . . .

'John. Sorry. I didn't mean the shirt. I wasn't really asking about your shirt. I mean, it's not important – '

His frown stayed. He looked puzzled. Then –

'I was already being prudent. I was eating cheaply.'

She had made the further mistake of laughing, for he meant it.

'From now on, from today,' he said, 'we will eat cheaply, and eat out rarely. We shall have to economize. We shall learn other and less indulgent ways of living.'

'Yes,' she said.

'Frugality is the key word, Helen. From now on. From today.'

'Yes, John,' she said, like a sweet little girl, but feeling a tiny itch under the band of the wedding ring she was still astonished that she wore. He looked at her suspiciously.

'A blessing in disguise,' he said, lifting his hand and then dropping it, leaving her unsure whether this was an old form of benediction or a new threat of violence. But then, at last, he had given her his beautiful, slow smile, and made everything all right again.

Which was why that strange homecoming had been so much less unpleasant than the scene in this room, The Work Room, five weeks ago.

A scene that had not ended in one of his old smiles. She had stayed where she was, by the door, watching him, unsure what to do. The grey in her eyes had gone more silvery, and then glistened with her terrible sadness and disappointment. He picked up his tweezer, and bent still closer over the first ring of sepals, taking not a blind bit of notice of her presence or grief. She understood, standing there, that there was no point in anger or resentment. It must be, it could only be, the soiled past which was taking him so far away from her: and moving out still further, in an orbit which would eventually take him out of her view, out of her life.

They had not made love since that day.

And here she was again, five weeks later, determined to force the issue, opening the door without knocking, breaking in on what he had made of his world.

Where was he?

The little eye on the coffee-machine still glowed red, and there was still coffee in its glass jug. A few cubes of cheese, perfectly shaped, and a couple of cream crackers, properly lined-up, remained on the crumbless plate at the far end of the bench. His drawing-board had white cardboard clipped on it, and his brushes had not been washed and placed in their grooves. It was clear that he had not finished for the day.

Seeing these things, her heart ached.

But then she wondered why she was being so precise in her observations. Anyone would think this was the *Marie*

Celeste, she thought, or the very different room with everything living in it that her father had left on the Sunday afternoon that he had died.

John must have gone out through the window door into the garden, or down to the pond. There was no need to make a mystery out of it. And yet that was what she was doing. Her heart was beating faster.

Something out of alignment in the feel or the look of the room, and some strange but strong instinct in herself, gave her the sense that he had not just stepped out to gather a plant or clear his head. He had 'disappeared'. *Vanished*, said her head.

Helen stood still, listening to the room, her head cocked to catch at what she experienced, illogically, as an alien presence. No: the echo, or the after-trace of one.

The faint, impossibly faint, and still receding sound of what was not exactly a cry in the air from far, far away, but which she could not have described more accurately, unless, analogously, with a shiver.

'John – ? she said.

5

Living in an enforced present tense is too much like being made to breast the rapids of a river. The attention has to engage with the racing white foam rather than the depths. By the middle of the churning and frothing evening, the newly made John Buck, an amnesiac in a fugue, was as heavy-limbed and exhausted as his body had ever been. He wandered up and down the strange streets around his hotel and the railway station, without a memory in his head longer than a day, but equipped with the bothersome impression that there was something very important he was supposed to do.

He had bought himself the basic toilet articles, a battery razor, a bottle of slippery-looking bath oil, green, which promised to awaken a recollection of something, somewhere, somehow, a few new shirts, socks, underpants, a small case to put them in, all the serious newspapers, and then the tabloids as well.

HUNT FOR CRAZED KILLER had no more appeal than the down-page THIS IS THE AXE-MAN, but a quick read showed that neither headline had any relevance to his own condition. He dropped the papers into a litter bin. The bin had a strip of paper stuck across it which said, in marker-pen ink, FRESH YOUNG MODEL 2 MINS AWAY 723, and the rest of the number torn off.

FRESH YOUNG MODEL detained him awhile. He was puzzled by the words. They seemed to him to signify something especial to do with the task, or the duty, or the sacrifice that had to be performed. The words gave him a metal taste at the back of the mouth, and as he walked on past the bin a lump of discarded hamburger on the pavement turned the taste into nausea, so that he had to stop a moment and take deep breaths.

He wondered what else he should buy, dismissing the obscure temptation to carry back a potted plant or a bunch of cut flowers to his room. There was no immediate cause to worry about what he was going to do when the money ran out. He still had an embarrassingly large of amount of money in his pocket. His previous self had prepared well for the successor.

The hours were being dismantled too slowly. His knees and his shoulders ached, and his head felt too heavy for his neck. The pavements were too hard for his feet, but he knew that he had to keep pounding along them. Seldom, though, did he walk far in any one direction, so he was never more than half a mile from the station.

What to do, what to do? The sights, the sounds and the smells had become an affront to him. But short of arson, mass slaughter, and a fleet of crop-sprayers adapted to send down thousands of gallons of the strongest possible disinfectant, there was no ready solution to the problem.

But he chuckled at the thought, until he caught a sidelong glance from another pedestrian.

Paddington is the low-tide stretch of a long-since beached city. Small hotels rub greasy shoulders in rows, adorned with romantic and exotic names, peeling plaster, grubby windows, and signs which reverse at the flick of a smirk from VACANCIES to NO VACANCIES. Worse cafés, manned by sallow waiters who wanted most of all to stand in the doorway. Cavernous pubs with overfilling ashtrays and Australian barmen. Late-night shops with daylight-robbery prices. Irish drunks. Arabs facing away from Mecca. Litter.

He was most of all irritated by the pervasive odour which seeped through the long straight street, especially now that dusk had settled on the buildings. Imagine something made out of dried and stale oregano, unwashed armpits, pub slops, and the sweat left on small change in a tight trouser pocket. That was what *he* imagined.

But if I cannot remember my real name, if I do not have any recollection of any detail from my own past life, then how is it – he reasoned – that I can distinguish between one smell and another, or remember how to tie my tie, or what newspapers to ask for, and what to do, what not to do in a thousand ordinary situations?

He would have to find a reference library, and look it up. Safer, perhaps, than going to some quack. Better by far than walking into a police station, and exposing yourself to – to –

In the middle of a stride, he stopped. What? Expose yourself to what? There is something I am afraid of, he thought. What had he done?

Oh, to be away from these doubts and frets! If only his head would clear, and the air would clean itself, and the streets did not go on and on with their filthy babble!

Before he moved again, he felt the depression gather itself up into one heavy ball of vapour and then drift slowly off him, clinging for a moment to his shoulders but unable to stay there, floating away, thinning into an ordinary layer of mist before disappearing into the buildings on the other side of the street.

He then saw, without great surprise, that although the outer cladding of these buildings remained in place and undisturbed, he was nevertheless able to see deep into their skins, and, by keeping his gaze fixed, even deeper, and deeper, right through to the inner cavities and the bowels and the creak and crumble of their corsets and bones, walls and stairways, beds and baths and kitchen appliances.

He held his breath.

The air pressed for release against the bones of his chest, and some of it rose to drum against the inside of his ears. As he finally let it go, in a small hiss of escape, room after room, floor upon floor, opened up further and further in a gliding motion of widening perception.

An old man, his clothes hanging slackly on his concave frame, a grey stubble on his chin and the damp remnant of a bent cigarette in his mouth, was peeing torrents into an already soiled trench of a sink. Across a hall, through another wall, a striped cat stretched itself out with a fat purr on a button-back settee which had a wooden alphabet brick perched precariously on the rolled arm.

Up a floor, but, oddly, getting nearer and nearer, a skinny young woman with long arms and big hands was pulling off a sweater and, while still entangled in it, kicking off the one shoe she was still wearing. At the same time, on the same floor, beyond the thicker dividing wall, a child in a sagging wet napkin shook the bars of its cot, in a red-faced, toothless rage.

There was, elsewhere, a fish in a bowl, a bird in a cage, and a sullen husband who looked like a dog in a manger.

Flickering boxes, here, there, and in many places, all showed the same passing image of a battered car hurtling along at a calamitous speed between a twisting and turning row of iron girders. It went on two wheels, overtoppled, and burst into a ball of flame. The picture, duplicated again and again and again, became a big can of baked beans.

He was still letting the air out, but the last pocket of it continued to press hard against his chest. *Let go*, he ordered his lungs *Let go. Let go!*

And out it went. He realized that he was not only getting nearer to the peeled-away rooms in the opposite buildings, but higher too.

Oh, this was a soaring game, with a soft riffle of air, a whoop inside and a swoop outside, and a rush in the ears, higher and higher. The dull, rain-like glint of the roof slates pitched at him, then passed under him, and momentarily gleamed in and out of his sight as he learned how to adjust to the weight of the dusky sky and the lightness of his own limbs.

He found out how to slow the whirl and whoosh of his flight, pull himself back, and hover briefly at the sashed and quartered windows. At one of them, the darker glass silvered and dissolved, and he could see a young woman in a tight dress at a door which was opened by a man in his underpants. He hovered in a watching position, saw the man give her a roll of banknotes, and her hand go down to his swiftly exposed genitals.

It was harder to see, now, and the window glass darkened but he was able to grab at the picture of the man putting his hands on her shoulders, steadily pressing down, until she knelt before him and allowed her mouth to enclose his penis. She looked at his hovering figure, and seemed to smile an almost shyly comical smile, telling him that she had been the woman throwing stones into the pond. That's not true, he thought.

He descended again, with only the smallest tilt and bump into his own shoes, here, back on the pavement, waiting for him.

Well, now. This was something else he had forgotten.

'I didn't know I could do that,' he said.

'None of us do, mate,' a sardonic voice said, at the side of him. A young man with lank hair was pushing by, giving that little twitch of the shoulders which, in the entire world, belongs only to London working-class males who imagine they have said something amusing.

John Buck instructed himself, yet again, to be more careful about keeping thought and speech apart. The injunction, delivered without his lips moving, had the secondary effect of restoring distance and solidity to the jumble of old buildings on the other side of the street.

'The things people do,' he thought to himself, with disgust, remembering what he had seen.

The buildings had put back their coverings, and the people within could hide away their infamy. But the structures remained gashed and bitten-into by windows and doorways and their own splashes of artificial light.

One such opening led straight up into a narrow and very steep flight of stairs. The sight of it pulled at him. The open door, the orange glow of light behind it, and the steps ascending into darkness or mystery had the shape and the emotional resonance of an illustration to a fable. Indeed, as he studied it from across the road, it looked as though the stairs *were* painted on the wall, but by someone who was indifferent to the rules of perspective and ignorant of the balances of colour.

He began to move his feet again, properly earthbound. The clack of his heels going hard down, drew him towards the doorway. The attraction was real, but he could not fathom it. A flow of traffic coming from the station held him up for a while, and he wondered why some of the cars tooted at him.

The doorway turned out to be the entrance to an unappetizing little hotel, whose rooms presumably spread over the adjoining shop and kebab house. An old, handwritten sign, to which a later Arabic had been attached, indicated that Reception was at the first landing of the steep flight of stairs. The stairs had no banister rail because the walls were not much more than a shoulder wide. It seemed to be a boarding house for anorexics and retired Gurkhas.

He could not summon up any image of the kind of clerk who would be sitting at the top of the stairs, which puzzled him a little, as he now understood that he could see further than he had previously thought. In compensation, though, he had a distinct enough impression of the man's eyes, which were unable to hide the contempt of the unspoken, 'Ho, so you've come to *this*, have you?' as he greeted those who wished to register.

There was a hot and oily stench of spiced meat down here on the pavement, and the elusive attraction which had brought him close to the door was no longer at work. He waited, behaving now under another command. His throat had dried itself out again, and he wondered why it was he could not plunge away, free of the stink of meat and the sight of soiled creatures passing up and down on the street. But he waited. He knew he had to wait, and that his agony would not last for ever.

There are times to fly, and times to plant your feet.

6

The suspended terrarium took on a sudden sheen as the sun burnt its way free of the clouds and angled through the windows. Helen did not feel its warmth. She was looking around the room, trying to locate the source of the chill which had whiffled past her, swaying her mind.

A faint smell from one of the plants scattered about the walls rode for a moment on the new gleam of light. Outside, the sun withdrew again, and the room stepped back into its old tinges. A flower moved its head, and she thought she heard one of the grasses sigh.

'*Stop it*,' she said to herself.

But the thought, aimed at an irrational anxiety, had the counter effect of suddenly pushing up into her reach the troubling dream of the previous night.

She remembered, now, how she had been clattering too fast, in heels too high and a skirt too tight, down the ludicrously steep pitch of some broken wooden stairs. The walls were closing in on her with a baleful and brown malice. A man was cursing her at the top of the steps, but whatever degradation she was trying to escape was less painful than what she was hurrying to meet.

John was on the pavement at the foot of the tilting stairs, waiting for her. He was standing legs apart with his fly unzipped to reveal the long, erect stem or shoot of a wild flower, which he held in his hand, with a wet-mouthed leer on his face. The hatred and contempt made a gasp stick in her throat. There he was, jeering obscenely at her, right in the middle of a harshly lit stretch of pitted and littered city pavement, poking and flapping the erect shoot of small yellow flowers at her, with no one passing seeming to care or even to notice.

'Where are your shears, you whore?' he cried as she reached towards him, in a plea for him to be as he once used to be, 'Where is your pruning knife?'

And that was it. Nothing else. A terrible accusation, but not much of a nightmare, as these things go.

She remembered now that she had broken awake with a clammy film on her skin, and a foreboding of dread. The moon was at the window, with a cold sneer on its yokel face. She had turned to touch John beside her, saw that his eyes were open and that his face had turned to silver, but before she could speak his name she had fallen asleep again. And blotted it out, until now.

Perhaps this, the unremembered dream, had been the secret cause of the chill which had fingered her in the room a moment ago?

Half relieved by her own answer, she went to the un-occupied bench. He had not gone so far in this odd isolation as actually to forbid her to look at his work, but he had not shown any of it to her. Each day, he locked the room when he finished, and put the key in his pocket. What was he up to? Maybe he was ashamed or unhappy about what he was doing. Perhaps the so-called Great Enter-prise which he had announced over a boiled egg the morning after losing his job was nothing more than a device, an excuse, a hidey-hole, for his new and strange introspection.

She stopped, and stared.

Two things were happening to her. First, she saw, belatedly, what her dream meant. Secondly, she saw, with her outward gaze, that his work was brilliant, and frightening.

Frightening because – and her eyes widened – the painting she was looking at was leaf, stem and bloom the self-same

46

flower which had featured so obscenely in the dream she had just recollected.

'How could he know?' sprang out of her.

But she knew this was a stupid thought. Coincidence was the word: coincidence, the useful force, the one which linked things without joining them together. It could grow anywhere, on any soil like some of the weeds around her in the room.

This plant, the one he was painting, the one in her bad dream, grew on the stone wall which partly surrounded their paddock, beyond the pond, on the edge of the up-and-down road from the house to the village. So there was nothing which could genuinely be said to be astonishing about its outcropping in her dream, nor was it (rationally) in the least surprising that the plant should flower here, too, on the stiff white card on the drawing board.

'Even so,' hummed her mind, 'even so . . .': as though it were unhealthily reluctant to give up a more mysterious explanation.

But where was he, anyway? What was he doing?

She studied the painting. One thing, at least, was strikingly clear: she did not need to worry about whether he was working properly. This piece was so much more than a mere copyist's art. The yellowy-gold blaze of the thick cluster of small flowers bunching together at the head of the tensely erect stem was alive with more than its own colour: it seemed to be caught in one of those swift changes between one light and another, a sense of chromatic movement which extended into a waver or a tremble in the plant iself. The flower looked to her as though it had been touched by the smallest breath of air; making it stir with what she felt was its own idea of itself.

Helen stopped chewing at her lower lip. She began to blush, which was rare, and which happened only when she was alone and unobserved. She didn't know whether her cheeks were tingling for pleasure or for shame. The skill and the act of adoration revealed in the small painting was far beyond anything she had ever seen or expected in his work. She could see, too, that the level of concentration such a task needed was enough to make anyone shut down his mind to most other things, and all interruptions.

'I know I can do it,' he had said, at breakfast the day after losing his job. 'I know my value, even if nobody else seems to.'

His egg was going cold, and he had not drunk any of his coffee. She had never before heard him justifying himself to himself in this way. It sounded dreadfully like bravado to her.

'There are no more lies to tell, thank God!'

She had looked up sharply when he said that. There would always be lies to tell if they were to be happy together. But he was talking about working in advertising, and not their past. Or was he?

'Wild flowers,' he said.

'Sorry?'

He had been drawing buttercups and daisies and a haze of meadow for some dairy by-product high in saturated fat. It had been his easiest and yet least discontented work, professionally, he said –

'I didn't know you'd ever been unhappy,' she had interjected, because his saying this made her feel guilty and threatened.

– and he knew a great deal about wild flowers and so-called weeds, thanks to his bloody old bore of a father, he said. Perhaps, at long last, the seeds of the florets had drifted into his mind, and were now taking root.

'The what did?' she asked, ready to laugh.

But he had kept talking, that morning, and she saw there was no saving glint of self-parody in his eyes, of the kind she knew so well. Not only were his sentences beginning to over-elongate and his manner to get up on stilts, but even his face looked as though it were about to change shape. More than solemnity had fallen on him, virtually within a single day.

She had listened, of course, and nodded, of course, and once or twice inserted what would normally be considered to be a smile of encouragement. He had taken no notice. All the time, as he ploughed on without touching his food or his coffee, she hoped that she was hearing nothing more than an example of one of the delusions, always soon abandoned, of those who have had their pride wounded or their safety threatened. She knew what it was like.

The working routine he had said he was going to follow – 'strictly, and without exception, and without interruptions' – sounded to her more like a punishment. An act of penance, maybe, to expiate the guilt he must be feeling as the suddenly jobless breadwinner. The white knight who had been thrown from his horse.

'This will pass,' she said to herself, hardly daring to sip her own coffee. 'This will pass.'

'So far as I can recall,' he was saying, the egg not touched but the spoon still in his hand, 'there are considerably more than two thousand different kinds of wild flower which might be considered as native to this country – '

'Goodness,' she had said. 'Are there?'

The blade of his look swathed across the table at her.

'I mean, that's a lot,' she added, nervously.

'Helen. Don't do this,' he said.

'Don't do what? What are you talking about? John. Why are you looking at me like that – ?'

'I can see very well that you do not wish to understand. I can see that you don't believe in what I am saying. That's all right. So be it. But I *will* ask you, please, not to show it in this way – '

'John?'

'I am not the patient. You are not the nurse.'

'John!'

'John nothing! Either support me, or say nothing at all! You've been simpering and nodding at me like a – well, I won't say like what!'

'You don't have to!' she spat.

He got up and left the table, nor had he turned back when she cried out. What he had been about to say, what in fact he actually *had* said, violently breached his own promise to her. She thought that she never would hear it from him, and it felt as though she had been hit in the stomach.

John had been gentle with her in all the important things. A man whose slowly stroked smile was part and parcel of his candour, his warmth, and his utter emotional reliability. She had never put it in so many words, but she considered that he had saved her from messy degradation, or death itself.

What could have happened? Why was everything going wrong?

She kept her attention on the picture of the wild flower he had been working on. It was not complete. The plant was shown on a dry-stone wall, which here edged off into the tentative. He had put his brushes down, as though the hardness and aridity of the texture had forced him to stop.

Where had he gone?

Unsure whether she ought to do so, Helen picked up the stiff white card on which the yellow flower was painted. She turned and turned it in her hands, as though she were hoping it would yield up some message.

On the other side of the card, the flower was named, in sharply pencilled letters, small and bristling neat. *Sedum reflexum.* Reflexed stonecrop. In the bottom right-hand corner was the number 927.

927? Had he done so many of these exquisite little things? Or did the numbering refer to something else?

A stack of filing cards was strung together towards the

back of the bench. Feeling vaguely criminal, but unreasonably so, Helen bit her lower lip again and riffled through the cards. Each one was covered in neat and tiny writing. Here and there, the sharp pencil had been pressed down so hard that it had dug a distinct groove. The dot of each i, especially, and the curl of most of the commas, seemed to have been engraved with an angry precision.

927. The number was biting. She wondered why. Perhaps it had occurred in her dream. Did it have any special significance?

'927' began the card, now that she located it in the stack. 'The bleeding of flesh wounds. Inducement of vomit. Ulcers. Sores and scabs on the skin,' and then, so different that it might have been written by another hand, a scrawl in sloping capitals said *KILL PENNY.*

She dropped the card and turned away, quickly, with an expulsion of breath. There were many more words on the index-card, reverting to their neat, lower-case, stick-insect march, but she did not want to read them. The sharp stabs of the pencil had already done their damage.

The faint and elusive odour had returned to the room. It wafted the beginnings of repellence into the odd chill that again seemed to eddy from one wall to the other. The row of plants by the big windows overlooking the garden began to shift and tick, and then, as though summoned by them, a fat and slow bluebottle came from nowhere to buzz and bounce heavily against the walls and, eventually, the glass.

Click! went the keep-hot coffee-machine. She jumped.

'I'm on edge,' she told herself, unnecessarily.

She wanted to leave the room, at speed, but instead she went to the garden windows, as though rehearsing the will and the sense that she would later be needing. The fly was going to be squashed.

But as she reached the window, she saw John through the glass, and she stared, and stared. The fly crawled and buzzed up the pane, but she neither heard nor saw it.

51

The window she was staring through looked out on a slope of lawn. The grass ran down to a gravel path, of the crunchiest kind, and a raggle-taggle row of the larger and more complacent shrubs. Beyond these was the stony remnant of an old outbuilding, and then, at a lower level still, a large pond fringed on its distant side by reeds.

That was where he stood, as still as a figure in a painting. His back was mostly to her, and it was not particularly hunched or drooped. But the overwhelming impression his position and his stance gave to her was one of his loneliness and despair.

He moved, stooped, picked up something, and then stood still again. She did not move, watching through the window as though held in a spell. It startled her when, suddenly, his arm looped out and tossed whatever he had in his hand into the middle of the pond. 'Plop!' it went.

A bird dived down and skimmed the water, then flapped away. It all looked as though it had happened in an arranged sequence, patterning melancholy.

'John,' she said, in no more than a murmur.

He turned, exactly as though he had heard. Even from this distance, and through the ripple of the thick old windowpane, she could see the tightness of his mouth and the glitter in his eyes. He stared the green and mottled length to the window, unyieldingly. She lowered her eyes in defence, and became aware again of the big fly as it bounced against the glass.

7

Seeping out from the half-empty kebab house with an undertow of animal pain and trampled vegetation, the over-powering stench of spiced meat and bubbling oil threatened to drive him off. But he kept manfully to his as yet un-explained vigil on the pavement, his arms crossed and his legs braced. It was not only the smell which afflicted him. Electronic rock music was beating out from somewhere near, in a pretence of male orgasm, splattering the street and the skins of the passing vehicles.

Guttural Arabic came up at him as three young men passed, bumping and barging. One of them laughed, and it sounded like a girl on a hockey field.

This is no good, hissed his brain. The smell, the noise, the people passing up and down in front of him. A scum left by the receding bilge. Stay here much longer and I shall have to hold my nose: but if I do, how can I stop my ears?

He shifted his weight from one foot to the other, and felt a tight cord loosen a little at the stretch of his knees. Oh, good, he thought, realizing that he was about to shed the pull of his flesh and bones and escape again. Wait, wait, there is no hurry, soothed another and calmer voice, not quite his own, and yet as much a part of him as his wings had been.

'Hello.'

He carefully unfolded his arms, and blinked.

'Hello,' he said, not sure whether it was proper to say anything at all.

'You want business?'

'I'm sorry. Do I want *what* – ?'

'A fuck. Or a suck. Anything else you fancy?'

The girl was mournfully thin and custard-pale, with heavy eyelids and a crimson gash of a mouth that almost lopped off the bottom half of her bony little face. He was astounded. All the filth, the noise, the smell of the streets had gathered itself up into a human form, and spoken to him.

She took his measure, switched off her eyes, so that they were suddenly those of a corpse, and kept waiting.

'A what?' he said. 'Do I want a *what*?'

He fell in behind her, his eyes on the exaggerated swing of her skinny hips. 'Hey,' he called.

She stopped, and gashed her face open again.

'This is not right,' he said to himself, making sure that his lips were folded into themselves. 'This cannot be the correct way to behave.'

'Change your mind?' she asked, simpering up at him.

'This cannot be the correct way to behave,' he said.

'Up you,' she said, and continued on her way.

He wondered if he should go after her again, take hold of her stick of an arm, and remonstrate with her. He had a handkerchief with which to wipe off the slippery red shine from her mouth, and he put his hand in his pocket to get it ready.

'No, no. That's not her. She's not the one.'

As he returned to the place where he had been waiting, he heard a swift click-clack of high heels coming fast down the steep stairs which led straight on to the pavement. The legs coming into his view were long and slender and vaguely familiar. His mind jumped to meet them, and he felt a kind of flowering at his loins.

It was a young woman with several thin bracelets jangling loose against her wrist. He watched her hesitate, look up and down, and then go four or five along to where a small sign with a missing letter flickered. PRIM–OSE, another cheap hotel, with a sign about as appropriate as KEEP OFF THE GRASS would have been, in both senses.

She disappeared into the doorway. He stayed where he was, his eyes fixed on the place she had entered. It was right to wait. It was the proper thing to do. He knew that now, for some of the tension had gone out of his limbs.

In less than five minutes she was back on the pavement again, looking up and down with the same hesitancy as before. Her fair and silky hair took on an additional shine from the street light, which had the pendulous droop of a flower growing in a stockade.

'Meadowsweet,' was the word which went *plop*!

He was unable to hear the soft tinkle of her several fine-spun bracelets from this distance, but he imagined the sound and it set up an answering vibration in his own chest bone. It seemed to him to be important not to let her out of his sight.

She was crossing the road, diagonally, against the traffic, towards a third and larger hotel, altogether more respectable, where the ground floor had been partly made over into a medium-slow, as opposed to a wholly fast, food dispensary. A large window showed the people eating in it, and the light so bright made them look performers on a suspended screen.

The passing traffic, and the flickering mask of their bodies, made it difficult to keep track of her. At one moment, she seemed to lose herself in a throng of off-duty basketball players, tall and black and bouncing. But then she was in the clear again, and in the meantime had pulled the sleeves of her closely fitted sweater half-way up to her elbows.

He liked, too, the intimate manner in which the black of her skirt clung to her legs as she walked.

'She is making patterns,' he thought, 'her legs are changing the shapes and the colours around her.'

And as he tilted his head to confirm the thought, he had a strong sense that a segment of his own past was about to detach itself from the dark oblivion and slide back into view. He flexed his mind to catch at it, determined not to lose hold in the way that he had with the dream.

The speck, for it was nothing more, blew off in the asphalt and lodged for a moment in his vision. A long bench spread out before him, gnarled and whorled with old wood, good to the touch. Sunlight flooded at a slant across it from a big sashed window looking out upon the slope of a lawn.

I am making colour with my fingers!

No. That was not it. He had something in his hand to help him, but it was the colour which was imposing itself on him, rather than the other way round. Yellow, pushing into a gold, bright and then darkening, with the movement of a living thing.

He was at first separate from the colour, observing it. But gradually it caught hold of him and sucked him into itself, and he was entering the folds, as a bee might, for yes, of course, this was the stuff of a flower. A cluster of yellow heads, beckoning him in, enclosing him, so that the erect stem which held them up also held *him* up . . .

Then everything went again. The stem, stiffening, was the last to go.

'Kill Penny,' he thought, and blinked, not understanding.

He stared anxiously across the street, looking for the girl, since she seemed to have a connection with what he had lost. She had disappeared. Much of the street itself had gone hazier, and the buildings opposite merged into and out of a lattice of half-forming, sliding, slipping recollection, as though the space in between was occupied by a glitter of water and then a line of silhouetting bushes and finally, in a blaze, the sun on window glass.

He thought, at first, that she was standing on the other side of the distant window, but the haze had cleared in time for him to see that she was on the move. It must be that she had gone into the third hotel and out again, as swiftly as with the others in the street. Sleeves pushed up, bracelets at her wrist, skirt tight against the sway of her, she was crossing the road to his side of it again, but further along, towards the railway station and the massive edifice of his own dignified and wholly respectable hotel.

He decided that he would go back to his room, in order to lie down. It was exhausting out here on the streets, and the city light was playing tricks on his tired eyes. The lamp standards pretended to be forms of vegetation, and the cruising black taxis tried to be the water in the pond. If he walked a little more quickly, he would catch her up, for he could see that her stride had slowed.

She was looking up and down again, in the same hesitant manner as before. It looked as though she were confused, or lost, searching for a place or a person she could not see.

8

Helen began calling his name as soon as her feet crunched on the gently descending loop of the gravel path. No man should be standing like that, alone and so obviously forlorn, aimlessly tossing small stones into the pond. It was as though he were throwing hard chunks of misery into the depths of his own thoughts. Besides, she needed to talk to him, feel his arms around her once again. She wanted to tell him how brilliant and beautiful were the little wild flowers he had kept alive on his white cards. 'KILL PENNY', and why he had written it, would come later, after she had penetrated his gloom and hostility.

For a few yards, at this angle, her feet crunch-crunching with the sounds of a healthy appetite on the dry gravel, she was unable to see all of the pond. As much as half of its oval was lost from view. She called his name again, as though afraid that he might disappear, but she called it lightly so as not to give him the idea that anything could be wrong.

Helen was passing under a great old tree with tealeaf-coloured leaves, the cause of the blocked view. The leaves were tired and dusty now with the burdens of an expiring summer, and ready for their fall. Their coppery spread made a kind of tannic shade on the path, but when the pattern of light changed at her feet she would be able to see whether he, hearing her call, was turning to greet her as so often in the past. His smile and his arms slowly opening.

'All right,' she said to herself, grimly, 'if he wants to throw stones into the pond like a little boy with the sulks, then we'll do it together –'

She stopped, abruptly, clear of the shade. He was not there. And yet, only a moment ago –

'John?' she called, again. She knew that he could not possibly be more than a few yards away. Not unless he could fly.

Her hand went up to her throat, quicker in its reaction than her mind. *God, I'm jumpy*, she acknowledged, making it go down again.

The greenish scum on the far side of the pond rippled suddenly, like the skin of an ancient reptile writhing free of the water. A wind was stirring in random eddies, and the big tree behind her moved within itself, with a reluctant hush and shush, a creature trying not to be awakened. Way above it, the heaped-up fleece had started to lose shape and race across the sky. She felt her hair lift a little, and her pulse quicken.

Helen looked back at the house. Interesting Early Victorian, their friend the estate agent had called it, with the professional knack of adding one adjective too many, and a banal one at that.

Acre House could have been named for the space it occupied, or for the bitterness it had experienced. The previous owner, she was told in the village, had hanged himself on the stairway, but the cord had snapped, so instead he had broken his back in the fall. It was his bank manager who found him, still alive, several hours later. They say he had called in order to discuss the overdraft, and had managed to do so before the poor man expired.

John claimed that he liked the tale, saying that it gave shape to a life, and that he himself would much rather be visited at the end by someone anxious to talk about money rather than God. One of the consequences, she presumed, of having had a clergyman as a father. Morbidity tends to run in families.

The house, at the moment, as she looked at it, certainly

suited what was alleged to be its recent history. When the sun was bright, it seemed to be shining out of the honey-coloured stone. But when the sky darkened and dipped, as it was doing now, the very same stones exaggerated the change. Helen thought that the house was at these times like a bad actor auditioning for *Wuthering Heights*.

She saw a light splash on the Work Room windows, tingeing the grass on the lawn beneath. The jump of the light from inside the house made her realize how quickly a gloom had mantled the garden.

He must have gone into the house through the back way, as she was coming along the gravel path under the now sighing and whispering tree. It made her alarm seem stupid. She could see his shape moving about in the light, advancing and receding. He was obviously busy again with his own things, going from the plants to the bench and then back to the plants again.

Helen stood still, and watched. She had a strong sense of their separation, or of her exclusion. Even as a child she had not liked looking into a lighted window at dusk, where other lives drew into themselves and shut her out in the gathering dark.

'The day thou gavest, Lord, is ended – ' the girls had sung, while the school windows turned to slate.

The wind was rising fast. It whiffled around her, and plucked at her. She stood still, letting it blow, and straining to hear the voice you could always hear in it if you were brave enough to listen.

What did it say?

He was out here by the pond, forlorn, and you were in there. And now he is in there, and you are out here by the pond, forlorn.

That is what the wind said. But not all at once. There were other thoughts in it, too, but they were not ready to be spoken. She turned her eyes away, and watched the topmost branches of the big tree ride in the darkening air.

Plop! went something in the pond behind her.

9

Helen had once and briefly thought about opening 'a little restaurant' of her own, which meant that she was not an especially good cook. She liked to think of herself as an imaginative one, though, and would no more dream of serving up such a debased compromise as, say, Chicken Kiev than she would of boiling small potatoes without their skins. The mustering, measuring and preparation of the ingredients for a meal was a balm to her, so long as she was not cooking for herself alone. A sidelong and edgily ambivalent flirtation with what she revealingly referred to as the 'new' feminist ideas 'in the air' had not so far introduced any severe qualifications or wounding ironies into her regard for her old-fashioned, blue and white kitchen.

Chip-a-chip-a-chop-chop-chop.

The sharp knife rocking in her hand, the herb shredding on the board, and a like maceration in her mind.

Chip-a-chop chip chop *chop*.

All day had been spent, it seemed, in the frustration or the bewilderment of flitting after his shadow. Irritation almost blanked out the pungency of the released odours. She was inflaming her nerves with the fret and the niggle-naggle of it all. The dancing blade was helping now, but not enough. The best thing about it, she thought, subversively, was that it was a weapon.

She had often had the image of herself backed up against a wall, with a knife in her hand. No, don't think of it! She concentrated fiercely and in fast strokes upon her irritation, rather than her fear.

John had been here, and there, and then nowhere, in and out of her reach like a winged creature. What on earth was the matter with him, or with her, or with every chop-chop-chop-chop thing? Time was when he sought her out, but now he was avoiding her.

The house was big enough to play hide-and-seek in until kingdom come, and old enough or queer enough to elaborate and wilfully complicate the search by its twists of leftover passage, variations of level, steps up and down and meaninglessly askew. There were unexpected alignments, as illogical as many a second thought, and alcoves with sudden blank stares, insolently refusing to acknowledge that they had been 'improvements' which had not worked. The place was full of all sorts of openings and closings, eels, ells, and ends. And these last few weeks were beginning to make her hate it. Lawns, paths, pond, outhouse and overbearing trees certainly included.

'Helen! Where are you?'

She stayed the knife, and stared down at her small white knuckles. His voice sounded angry, and bewildered. For some reason, she kept tight hold of the handle.

The shout had come from the floor above, from their bedroom or the long upper hall beyond it. She found it difficult to locate the usual resonances of the house, because he did not usually call like this, or indeed shout at all.

'Helen! Answer me! Where the hell are you?'

Where the hell do you think? Where I ought to be when people are coming to dinner. Oaf!

She surprised herself with the force of her own anger, dropped the chopping knife with a confirming clatter, wiped her hands vigorously on her pinafore, and yelled back.

'I'm in the kitchen!'

There were parts of the house where you could make yourself heard, quite easily, and yet not be able to hear back. It only increased her irritation to know that she was on the wrong end of one of these channels.

63

Pinafore still wrapped around her hands, she went out into the hall, and to the bottom of the long curve of the main stair.

'Why are you shouting?' she called up.

And then, when there was no answer, and because she might as well: 'Where have you been? What do you think you're playing at! John?'

Still there was no answer. Frowning, she looked up the flight to where the steps turned into dusky shadow. Was he going to start the peculiar and maddening catch-me-if-you-can all over again?

'Where's my knife?' she thought.

'John!' she yelled, full-throated, determined to put an end to all this nonsense.

He came partly into her view on the stair, the light poor behind him, and stared down towards and yet not quite at her.

'Helen?' Almost as though she were a stranger.

She was shocked, by his wavering gaze, by his voice, and by the expression on his face. Her hands stopped moving under the lifted pinafore.

Get the knife! she thought, in a sudden whoosh of fear.

He made a faltering gesture on the stairs above her, like someone trying to point at a blur too far away and too fast to be picked out, then slowly dropped his hand to his side and shook his head, defeated.

'What is it? What has happened?' she said, in not much more than a whisper.

'Helen – !' It was the worst of croaks, and his face had the glazed look of total bewilderment.

Released from her first shock, she started to run up the stairs. He suddenly stiffened, the glaze went off him, and his hand came up again, decisively this time, the palm straight and flat towards her.

'No!'

She stopped, her eyes wide.

'No. It's all right,' he said, in a normal tone. 'I would rather you didn't.'

'John. What's the matter? Are you feeling ill, or – '

'Ill?'

'You look as though you've seen a – You don't look very well.'

'Ill?' he said again, frowning at her.

Then he shrugged, dismissing the question, and turned away with a quick thump of his shoes, back up the receding curve.

'John!' she yelled.

He stopped, a few steps further up, and turned around to look back. For a moment, it seemed to her that he was about to smile his old, slow smile.

'Weren't you taught,' he said, instead, 'that it is rude to shout?'

'What?' she said, incredulous: and then, in a shriek, 'Fuck you!'

'And fuck you, too,' he answered. 'A more general invitation.'

He whirled about and continued on his way to the top, going out of her sight into the long upper hall. The remaining light had made the outside window look opaque at the far end of the hall. He was pulling himself along the wooden floor in a slow and heavy hunch of his tall frame, his feet clumping on the boards. A shaft of orange lampglow had angled out across the floor and on to the wall from one of the partly opened doors between him and the far window.

Reach it. Reach it, cried his mind, in an agony of fear.

But the subdued pattern on the walls, and their stretch away from him, had another perspective too. The light from the door up ahead, the whirling grey sky pressing into flatness at the window at the end of the corridor, the slight creak of the boards beneath his feet, all were suggesting or even trying to become other things, other sights, other sounds, and other voices. His head itself, receiving and distorting, seemed to be doing the same.

Reach it. Reach it!

He knew that it was vital to get to the door before the other world finally asserted dominion over him. Vital, vital, to reach the glow that was held back by the swing of the door and the crackle of its nerves. If he could go through, and lie down on the bed, with his face against the soft plumpiness of the pillows . . .

But who was calling out to him? And why was the sound of her voice so sad?

It was as close to him as the tingle of nerves threading on his own skin, and yet also so far, far away that it was beyond recovery. He knew, in a flash of revelation, that the call he had heard was from the woman in his dream. She was standing by the pond of black water, throwing polished black stones into it as a bird dipped and rose in a flutter of wing. There was a child there, too, with a blankness where the face should have been.

How odd and unnerving it is, he thought, how a dream can cling and fold itself around you, like a sheet of old newspaper blown against a lamp-post, and caught there until the wind slackened. Let it go. Let it drift.

He was puzzled for an instant by a subdued rumble, long and low, which was coming up through the stones beneath his shoes. There must be caverns down there, hidden from him, in which the thunder rolled, and the walls glistened with secret rain. Then, taking stock, and putting down the excesses of his imagination, he understood that the rumble was coming from an underground train, leaving the other part of the station which he could see in front of him.

Remember, then, that there are people at all levels here in this squalid place, he told himself, feeling his teeth to be as sharp and alien as fragments of stone against the soft flesh of his tongue. You had to be able to skim the surface froth and scum off things, to scrape away the dirt, peel back the folds or the skins, and peer as bravely as you could manage into the empty heart of the so-called solids. These structures all around, the street, the buildings, perhaps even the people crawling up and down like flies on the window-pane, they are all pretence, all make-believe. Be alert! he warned himself. Do not be hoaxed into error, embarrassment or something even worse by these masks and guises.

There was still so much to learn, but at least he was starting with a clean slate. His mind had rubbed away all the marks left by memory. He had no impediment that he could think of now which could stop him from finding the reasons for everything, the purpose that informed life. Discover it, follow it, accomplish it. Then he would feel good inside again, and be able to fly away once more, soaring free of the dirt and the decay and the warrens of betrayal.

But who was calling? Why was the cry so sad, and so close, and so far away? These traces of what must be his earlier existence were too thin or too fleeting to be anything other than an irritating ache. Better, by far, to concentrate on what was directly in front of his eyes, and to deal with life as it unfolded second by second, minute upon minute.

Thus, the orange glow of a hidden lamp, which had so elusively hinted at a door opening on to a long and glooming passage, was nothing of the kind. There was an evening-newspaper stand in front of it. It was, of course, the pavement which gloomed and deadened as the flagstones stretched away beyond the line of shops, the fast-food hovels, and the frosty-eyed public house. He had walked this way before, earlier in the day.

He saw her again, the hesitating girl, standing out clearly among the slop and sludge of bobbing heads and shoulders. Her hair had a way of attracting the street light, pulling down the shine into itself. She was motionless, with everything else around her in a continual fleck of movement. Even the wire-thin bracelets held their place against the slope of her long wrist.

She had been in and out of three hotels since he had first noticed her, and he could therefore assume that she was looking for a room and had so far failed to find one. The hotels she had tried were not what he would call expensive. Dirt cheap was the right term. He let his mouth smile. There was less need now to keep such a tight control of his face.

'Do you need any help?' he said, coming up on her, and speaking straight away, before he had worked out what he ought to say.

'Are you speaking to me?' she said. It was an Irish voice. He did not think he liked Irish voices, but had no idea why. But who else did she think he was speaking to?

'I am indeed. I simply enquired whether you were in need of assistance.'

'What do you mean?'

'It's just that I happened quite by chance to see you go into and rather swiftly out of several hotels back there, and though I have no wish to be impertinent – ' he tried to stop the words spilling, but they insisted upon the adumbrations, and his neck stiffened, ' – and I hope most sincerely that you do not imagine for one moment that I am attempting to chat-you-up, as I believe it is called in vulgar – '

'What?' she interrupted, at last.

'Parlance,' he said, and stopped, with a swallow of air.

She looked at him with an expression that would have been the ideal illustration for the first but no other page of a language instruction manual: I know the sounds you are making, one by one, as they come out, but it is beyond me to follow their sense from even a little way behind . . .

Bewilderment served to soften the edge of her face, which close to like this, was disappointingly sharp. When she had first swivelled and stared, with a small chink and tinkle at the end of her arm, he thought he had made a bad mistake. But he could see now that in most lights at most times she would be considered attractive.

He waited, patiently, for her to catch up with the sense of his words.

'I'm trying to get a hotel for the night,' she said, in her up-and-down brogue, and telling him only because it seemed to be simpler than any further attempt at decipherment.

'Ah,' he said, 'that is precisely what I had gathered.'

'But it's shocking the prices they are asking,' she said, not sure whether they were talking about the same things.

'And not worth it, I can assure you.'

'What?'

He sighed. The woman was stupid. 'Not worth it,' he repeated.

'That's what I said,' she said, frowning at him.

He nodded, and touched her arm, attracted by the tension between its roundness and its firmness. She pulled away, quickly, so her bracelets once again clashed against each other.

She was not the one. She was not the right girl. But he was tired, and hungry in a way that he did not understand. Besides, she was the right height, and had a similarly grace-ful figure, as the woman he had hoped she might prove to be. Plop! went a small noise in his head.

'I beg your pardon,' he said, with an obvious indignation. 'I think you entirely misunderstood the reason why I have approached you.'

Her green eyes blinked at him again, and her arm sent out another tinkle-tinkle.

'What?'

'What? What? What?' he said, holding back a worse jeer.

'What – ?'

'Forgive me for pointing it out,' he said, 'but you do say,

What? rather a great deal, you know. I take it that you do understand English?'

She gazed back at him. He smiled at her.

'I have the idea,' he continued, 'that you are a stranger here.'

'I haven't been over here before,' she said, as though she were contradicting him.

'Well, now.'

'Well, what?' and she sounded wary.

'Do you have the money and they haven't got the room? Or do they have the room, and you don't have the money?'

'What do you want?'

'I would like to help you if I can.'

'What for, Chuck?' she asked, with a hard edge.

'I could say it's because I like the way your bracelets jangle,' he said and laughed. 'But that wouldn't sound very convincing, would it? I could even say I like the *lilt* of your walk, but that wouldn't be the reason either. No. A helping hand, my dear. Simply a helping hand.'

She was examining him as he yammered on. He had a nice smile. He wasn't bad looking. He was wearing good clothes, but very old-fashioned: a suit. And he sounded like a respectable person.

'What sort of help?' she asked, and tried on a flirtatious smile which was not easy for her.

'I stopped to talk to you because I don't think you have any idea of the danger you are in.'

When she is startled, he noticed, her eyes have a green tremble in them, like the light on a leaf after rain.

The sudden fresh gleam hurt him, a knife in the chest, and he turned his head away but found that, no matter how much he twisted his face, he was still looking at her. She was somehow still there in front of him, with her greening, greying eyes, and the eyes were vivid with fear.

'Oh, Christ,' he moaned, 'oh, Jesus Christ.'

He did not know how he had managed to get through the door and on to the bed, and could not work out the angle of his sprawl across the top of the duvet. It was almost as though he had been somewhere else.

These dreams were becoming so overpoweringly real that the beat and flutter of them stayed in the room, drifting too slowly off to the corners and lingering there. If only he could get a proper heft on them, pull them back and look into them.

'John. Please.'

She watched his eyes stop flickering about and settle on her.

'Please, John. You are worrying me. What is it? Why are you behaving like this?'

He studied her.

'I don't think I know what you are talking about,' he said, slowly, and with great carefulness.

Each of them heard the clock strike across the fields and the September dusk from the squat-towered church in the village, less than a mile away, and too distant not to be melancholy.

'You called me,' she said, in a tone as level as his had been. 'I was in the kitchen starting the dinner, and you were up here somewhere.'

'Yes.'

'I came out into the hall, and you were on the stairs.'

'Go on. What about it?'

Helen sat on the bed, beside him. She went to take hold of his hand, and saw him stiffen and then, too late, try to hide it. She did not take hold.

'What about it?' he asked, in a grating voice.

She stood up, and moved away, towards the still partly open door. 'You know the Stoners and Angela are coming, don't you?' she said. 'And I hope you know what time it is.'

'I heard the clock.'

'I've got to get on with the cooking.'

'Yes,' he said.

She went on out, shutting the door. He heard her feet on the floorboard of the upper half as they quickened suddenly, and then as they stopped.

He waited, holding his breath.

Her steps began again. It was all right. They were going the other way. Thank God! She was not coming back into the room.

10

The conversation through the dinner had not been as free or as amiable as it should have been between friends of the same age and district. A number of small silences in which the cutlery sounded, a few over-deliberate switches of subject, and one too many congratulations about the quality of the layered terrine or the threads of orange in the basmati rice, had given Helen a small, tight headache.

'I cooked the bloody stuff,' she thought. 'Do I have to do all the talking as well?'

But now that the brandy was out and most of the plates cleared away there were signs of increased conviviality. Perhaps it was the pudding which caused Angela to bring up the subject of schooldays. They agreed, around the table, securely grown-up, that one of the nastiest of all regular dreams was where you found yourself back behind a desk in a classroom being asked a question which you had no idea how to answer. Then other terrors of the same provenance, drawn out of their various infancies, began to restore the animation and the laughter with which the meal had started. John, only, kept himself apart, with just an occasional nod or grunt to show that he was there at all.

They were all English, John and Helen, Martin and Clare, and Angela, and they had all reached their thirties. That is, they had come in their pale fashion upon the one stretch of their lives where it was possible for them to talk with a fair degree of accuracy about their childhood days. Later on in their years, and the twin national affections of nostalgia and morbid sentimentality would roll in upon them like the mists

73

of October, softening all the hard outlines, and turning pain itself into a sort of ambiguously defined silhouette. Any earlier in their lives, they would have been too busily engaged in that long withdrawal which the English call Growing Up.

Helen told them about being the sleeping princess in the middle of a ring of linked hands, a singing game. Martin Stoner said that when he was at primary school no boy would have dared to join in such fun, because of the scorn of the other boys and the potential enmity of the girls, 'who could be incredibly tough'. One little girl had once threatened to strangle him, he claimed. The only thing a seven-year-old boy who didn't like rough-and-tumble could do was skulk off on his own. With a 'secret friend': someone invented for the occasion.

'Oh, yes, I had one of those, too,' said Angela, in her languid drawl. 'Imaginary friends are so much braver than real ones. Mine lived in an absolutely enormous cupboard we had at the top of the stairs. It was a very dark cupboard.'

'Most children who have no one to play with,' said Martin, 'and parents who are too poor or too mean to give them enough toys – '

'Not mine,' Angela said sharply.

'Most such children,' Martin reiterated, with a glint as he looked across the table at her, 'are bound to end up inventing an imaginary friend, in or out of a cupboard.'

'That's not the reason,' she said.

'And as is so often the case,' he finished, smacking his lips in pleasure, 'what is so often thought of as a rich imagination is in actual fact nothing more than a defence against deprivation.'

He leant back a little, making the chair tilt, with the air of a man who thinks he has delivered himself of an aphorism. Martin was an estate agent, severely tempted to compensate for the floridity of his working language with an allegedly vigorous precision in his social one.

'That's nonsense, Martin. Utter bosh,' said Angela.

He smirked at her and lifted his eyebrows, but allowed the chair to right itself on all four legs.

'You're just playing with words,' she said.

'As usual,' said Clare, his wife, with a lift of her chin.

Martin frowned at Clare, and then tried not to, passing it off by rolling the brandy around in his glass and then swallowing some, falling silent under the cover of savouring it.

Helen looked around the table and hoped that the conversation was not going to slip back into awkwardness again. The day had been bad enough already without it having to end dismally as well. She felt such a sense of strain that it was difficult to think of anything to say, except sorry. But why should she say that? Whose fault was it?

Her eyes once again sought out John, who was still as mute as a snowman on the far side of the white tablecloth. She had long since subdued herself into the social graces for his sake, and learnt to smile and nod and swallow down the words she would once have used. It suited her well, when he was part of it. But tonight he had been embarrassingly silent and abstracted through most of the meal. Once or twice he had even been gross enough to sigh deeply, and privately, when they were talking about the effects of acid rain on the Black Forest or whatever it was.

'Well, this never happened to me,' Clare was saying. 'My problem always used to be how to find a space where I could be on my own. Damned if I was going to make up a pretend-friend when I spent so much time trying to get away from the real ones.'

'Me, too,' said Helen, with a laugh. In order to keep it going.

'Ah, but you had brothers and sisters, both of you,' said Angela. 'I was an only child, and there were no children next door either.'

'Precisely!' beamed Martin, with undue satisfaction. 'That's the exact point I was making.'

'No, it wasn't,' said Angela, with an equally inappropriate aggression.

He put out his tongue at her, and then looked sideways at his wife. And then everyone knew, if they hadn't guessed before, that Angela Graham and Martin Stoner had had other conversations in other places which no one else was supposed to discover.

There was a small silence. Angela, the brighter of the two, instinctively realized that neither of them should be the next one to speak.

Martin spoke. 'What's the matter, Angela?' he asked, with a passable imitation of a chuckle. 'Don't you like me, or what?'

'Like you?' said his wife, with a plunge of her eyes.

Angela could have struck him. Oh, the bloody fool, the absolute idiot! Grinning sheepishly across his raised brandy glass at her, in the same kind of awkward simper he had used to proposition her for the first time a few months ago.

'I see,' thought Helen, her interest considerably quickened.

'You rotten little shit!' thought Clare.

'Bloody nincompoop,' thought Angela.

'Clever old me,' thought Martin.

'I thought at first it was the cat,' said John.

They looked at him.

'We had a cat called Toby. The colour of the ashes in the grate after a fire had been kept in.'

They looked at each other.

'I used to talk to Toby. He knew what I was saying and what I was thinking. Or so I thought. But it gradually dawned on me that this was not the case. I suppose that once too often the damned creature curled itself up and went to sleep in the middle of a particularly complicated conspiracy

of mine. Or simply walked out of the room with its tail
straight up in the air. You know, the way cats do, showing
you a very contemptuous, perfectly round little bum hole.'

Angela laughed, mostly because she was nervous about
what had preceded John's incomprehensible speech.

'You must remember,' John said, frowning at her, 'that I
was marooned in a vicarage in a very small village in Norfolk
with a very large church and nothing very much else. Nothing
to break the horizon, all flat, so flat – '

'John,' Helen said.

'Nothing,' he said, sounding frighteningly bleak. 'For
miles and miles and miles in every direction.'

'John,' Martin said, with the remnant of his smirk still on
him, 'would you mind telling us what on earth you are
talking about?'

'A secret friend,' said Clare, with an edge.

'Oh. Back to that, are we?' asked Martin, belatedly aware
that, somehow or other, something had been let slip.

'We never left it,' Clare said, and looked at Angela, who
looked down into her coffee-cup.

John sighed to himself, and shifted in his seat, not listening.

'When the cat failed me,' he said, as though to himself, 'I
had to find another friend. I had to have a more reliable
comforter and fellow conspirator. But I had to call him up out
of nowhere. He came to me out of nothing, walking across
the flat fields and over the thorny hedges. It's a wonder he
ever found me, but find me he certainly did.'

He tapped a fingernail against his glass, again and again.

'Well, there's no need to sound so sad about it,' Helen said,
in an attempt at lightness.

Tap-tap-tap went the edge of his nail. Then –

'He came everywhere with me, once he had found me, and
I couldn't have shaken him off, even if I'd wanted to. I tried it
once, just to see what would happen. I ran and I ran, as fast as
I could, but when I had to stop, out of breath, he was there,

77

too. He ran where I ran. He walked where I walked. He sat next to me at the table, and, I tell you, he put the same food in his mouth, and he swallowed it down at the same time as I did.'

Helen could see that the others were uncomfortable, and she tried to signal to him with her eyes. He ignored her.

'He climbed the stairs with me, step by step,' he continued, in the same oddly remote tones, 'and he lay himself down in the bed beside me.'

'Oh, did he now?' Martin laughed, but he was clearly as uncomfortable as the others.

'He was at my comings-in and goings-out,' said John, in his father's voice.

Helen made an effort to stop him.

'We've got the picture, John,' she said. 'Don't go on about it, please, or we'll think you are – '

'There was not one single thing,' he said, raising his voice a little, the only sign that he had heard, 'not one that I did which he did not do. There was not one single place I went where he did not go.'

And then he looked at them full on at last, at each of them in turn, with the light of challenge in his eyes.

'What is the matter? What is all this about?' the three dinner guests asked themselves.

'More coffee. Anyone?' asked Helen, who wanted to cry.

Angela had at first welcomed the deflection of interest which John's peculiar narrative had caused, but now she could see a distress that fascinated her for its own sake.

'This make-believe friend of yours – ?' she asked. 'How long did he stay around? I mean, how old were you before you gave him the heave-ho . . . ?'

She bit off the words, for his violet gaze was now too fiercely upon her. She was astonished.

Bloody hell, she thought. *The man is mad.*

Tap-tap-tap went his nail on the rim of his glass again.

'What was his name, this friend of yours?' asked Clare, but looking at the others.

He lifted his hand away from the glass, but kept his finger crooked.

'John,' he said, shifting the tense. 'His name is John.'

11

On Thursday afternoons, rain or shine, the vicar would retire to an ingle of a room to write his sermon for the Sunday. The Sermon Room, as it came to be called, smelled strongly on low cloud days of St Bruno, and much of the rest of the time of some sort of liniment or embrocation. St Bruno was not a forgotten martyr or father of the Church, but a pipe tobacco. The embrocation, with its vaguely evangelical redolence, better suited the tone of the compositions which laboured on to the page. The room was a place which even the summer insects seemed to avoid.

The vicar was a bore and a bully, but he was not a morose man. He frequently made cheerful noises, and sometimes clapped his hands loudly, for no apparent reason. And when he wrote his sermons he tended to hum the tunes of his own childhood, and many a nursery rhyme as well.

Half a pound of tuppenny rice, half a pound of treacle, that's the way the sermon went, as he hummed and twitched and inscribed large capital initials for such words as Eternal and Way and Blessed. Half-way through, he would light his pipe, lean back with a crack of the wooden chair, billow a bit, bubble the stem a little, ponder a while, and then return to the lined paper with all the zest a new metaphor had given him. Pop, goes the weasel.

On Thursday evenings, immediately before supper and mugs of hot cocoa, half milk and half water, the sermon (similarly constituted) would be read aloud to his wife and his son. The delivery was accompanied by the same number of open-palmed gestures he used in the pulpit, and a few more of the ones which needed a pointed finger. From time to time, he would look up quickly from the page in order to catch any errant attention.

'Ih ill Oah-nn,' John's mother would say.

The boy had no difficulty in understanding that this meant, 'Sit still, John,' just as he had no problem in following her when she read to him on one night of the week, seated beside his bed. 'The badger's winter stores, which indeed were visible everywhere, took up half the room,' would have been made almost incomprehensible by her badly cleft palate to anyone other than himself.

'Ih ill Oah-nn!'

The smallest fidget or waver of his eyes, and he was caught. His father's speech had no impediment, but the boy had much more difficulty in making sense out of it. The words came rolling at his head in a deep boom-boom, enunciated with relish. An involved pursuit through labyrinthine metaphors, which ensured that John was lost by the end of the first few long sentences. And when on winter evenings the rain made its frying-pan noises at the window, and the unhindered Norfolk winds launched themselves at the impertinent extrusion of the house, the boy, sitting bolt upright, endured agonies of boredom as the sermon too slowly unravelled.

Father had one other hobby beside his pipe and its accoutrements. He liked to collect, label, and make spidery notes about what, characteristically, he called 'the small and unregarded blooms of the English hedgerow'.

Many of these would subsequently flower in his prose, but only to wilt and shed their colours in the drought of the dry thought and the tangle of subordinate clauses in which they were bedded. His expeditions to collect the flowers seemed to be journeys in search of a revelation that was unfortunately too humdrum to open any buds in the minds of his listeners.

'How many times have you passed by an unremarkable hedge at the boundary of a perfectly ordinary field,' he would boom to his audience, 'perhaps full of your everyday concerns, your eyes scarcely able to see what there is to be seen in even the humblest corner of the Lord God's Loving Creation? How many times in the course of a day spent out in the fresh air, whether in honest toil or healthy exercise, striding upon the highway, how often have you had occasion to see – perhaps without a thought – the bright yellow flowers of *Tanacetum vulgare?*'

He would then look over the top of his spectacles with what he knew to be an amused twinkle. 'And what, I can hear you ask, what is *that* when it is at home? What is he on about now?'

They were not asking any such thing. If any in his small and suitably pinched-looking congregation had been allowed to say a word, it would not have been to enquire after *Tanacetum*.

'*Tanacetum vulgare*, as our good friends the botanists call it – ,' boom-boom-boom, just as it always was on the previous Thursday evening, this time in a room made stuffy by the slow smoke from a banked-down coal fire in the grate.

He had looked over the top of his spectacles at his seven-year-old son.

'Ih ill Oah-nn!' said mother sharply, misunderstanding the break in what only its author would have called the sermon's flow.

'No, no,' murmured the Vicar, who knew that the boy had not moved, but did not suspect that his wife it was who had not been paying attention.

'*Tanacetum vulgare*. I wonder, John, if you happen to know what that is in its, shall I say, everyday dress? What is it called? I ask because I happened to mention it to you on our little walk the other day.'

John screwed up his face in an imitation of hard thinking.

'Um,' he said, his insides knitting with panic.

'Please don't say um. Never say um. You are not a bumble bee.'

These were the worst moments in the worst evening of the week. The questions aimed at him, the eyes settling on him from over the top of the glasses, and then the expectant and solicitous smile gradually fixing, and disappearing into a disappointed glower. It didn't matter how much he screwed up his face, and clenched his hands, and tried, and tried.

'The answer is not up there, now is it? I doubt whether you will find it written up on the ceiling, will you, John?'

John lowered his eyes and appealed to his secret friend, the other John, who had so far been ominously silent in the shadow.

'Take no notice,' said the other John.

'I distinctly recall pointing the flower out to you on the verge beside the road, beyond the broken gate you were attempting to swing upon,' his father was saying, rattling the paper in his thumb and finger.

'Ry Oah-nn,' urged his mother, telling him to try, and her eyes willing him to, and her hand fluttering to her face and back again.

'Doesn't matter,' said the other John, close at his ear now.

'All right. All right,' his father shifted in the chair. 'A clue. I will give you a clue, my boy. Small yellow flowers in a cluster. Each flower flat on the top, in what we call a disc shape. Mmmm? Mmmm? And if that doesn't give it away, then may I ask you to address yourself to the *smell*? Mmmm? Mmmm?'

The vicar tapped the side of his nose.

'It's full of snot and bogeys,' said his secret friend. 'It's full of hairs and snot.'

His father stared and stared, and John could hear the clock ticking throatily out in the dark brown hall at the bottom of the dark brown stairs.

'Feverfew,' he said, at last, without much hope.

'Feverfew,' said his father, in the mildest of tones, 'is basically white. A white flower.'

'Yes, Father. White. I am sorry, Father.'

A continued stare, impossible to deflect, and then a sigh like a small shudder, and a roll of his eyes at his wife.

'Tansy,' he said, 'the name is tansy.'

'Yes, Father. Tansy. I remember now.'

'I think, John, that you hardly deserve to share the supper table with us this evening. Perhaps it would be best, when you have heard and, I hope, inwardly digested the rest of this little piece, if you took yourself off to your bed, my boy.'

'Yes, Father.'

'But I don't want you to think of me as an unreasonable person, John. I want you to ask yourself whether it is fair, whether it is just. Wouldn't you say so? Mmm?'

'No,' said the secret friend, with an affronted bellow.

'Yes, Father.'

A nod, a slight hum, and a click as he brought his teeth together, and the sermon continued, after a wholly mannered and unnecessary, 'Where was I? Where was I? Ah. Yes.'

Another ten minutes of boom-boom-boom – but, mercifully, no more questions, except the usual quota of rhetorical ones – and he had reached what he made obvious to be the point of the sermon.

Tansy – 'and I am sure some of you will remember your mothers baking tansy cake at Eastertide' – had got its name, in a corrupted or diminished fashion 'from the Greek'. The original word, 'the hidden root' as he called it, once more looking over the top of his spectacles, was Immortality. Eternal Life.

John's father was the only Englishman he had ever met who pronounced 'eternal' in the same chilling manner as a Scottish presbyter would, ending an elongated second syllable with a roll of the 'r' like coal being emptied into a cellar.

'The old people, all down the ages, believed that an infusion of this plant, the self-same bloom you can see

84

yellow under the hedges, would when sipped give them eternal life.'

The congregation would recognize, with relief, that there was not much more boom-boom left in the locker. John, hearing it three days earlier, also had sufficient experience of these things to know the end was near.

'But they were wrong, of course. The gift they were seeking comes not from infusions, concoctions, human brew or bluster, tricks or devices. Eterrr-nal Life may indeed be given to us along the way, but only, dearly beloved brethren, only as we journey along one especial and narrow way. The one laid down for us, made ready for us, clearly signposted for us, by . . .'

Guess who. Our Lord Jesus Christ the Saviour.

'No, no, not him,' hissed the other John.

Our Lord Jesus Christ. Up the stairs, slow, reluctant, with no supper, no apple and raisin pie, Our Lord Jesus Christ, up and then around the turn with the squeak on the tread, eleven more steps, lift the metal latch, Our Lord Jesus Christ, and into the room with the steep slope on its ceiling, down to the little square window that looked on to the pitch of roof tiles, Our Lord Jesus Christ fading back into a distant boom from downstairs.

'Bloody,' said the other John. And then, 'Bugger!'

John climbed into his bed, impressed, and grateful that his secret friend could say words he himself would never dare to let enter his mind, and could never get within his own mouth.

'Shhh-shhh!' he whispered, holding down a guilty snigger.

'Do not neglect to say your Prayers, John,' came his father's voice, up the stairs. He pictured the head cocked for his response.

'No, Father,' he called.

He waited with a flutter in his chest for his friend to pronounce, as they both pulled up the bedclothes, smoothed the eiderdown, and settled down into the bed.

'Shit,' said his friend, and then made a farting noise.
'Our Father which art in heaven – ' John began, timidly.
'Don't!' said his friend, and farted again.

12

When she is startled, he noticed, her eyes have a green tremble in them, and the sudden fresh gleam went into him like a skewer. 'I have felt this before,' he thought, to assuage the pain of it. 'I have lived this moment in my other self – '

'*What?*' she said, the light in her hair, and still in front of him, and alarmed by whatever it was he had said.

He glanced quickly up and down, to get his bearings, and to bring back whatever he had wanted to say.

'These streets,' he said. 'Look at them. Take a good look. Any young woman on her own, walking up and down, and so obviously unsure of where to go or what to do – well! Don't you realize what sort of women frequent these streets?'

'What do you mean – ?' she asked, understanding enough of what he was saying to be offended.

'And the filth that preys on them,' he said, raising his voice. 'The pimps can't be far away, can they? I've no doubt they are lurking! What if they try to get their hands on you?'

She was trying to work out, and quickly, what measure of offence was appropriate. This man might be genuine, and therefore helpful. He was not necessarily a creep, for all the funny words that came out of him. But he was also saying, in effect, that she could be mistaken for a woman of the streets, one of the skinny slags she had seen a few minutes ago. Mother of God, if she was going to take money for doing it, she wasn't going to sell herself, was she?

'I'm sure I don't know what you mean,' she said, with the compromise of half a glower, capable of further adjustment either way.

He made himself hold his hand back from the soft curve of her arm.

'Well – you don't seem able to find yourself a room, do you? Where are you going to stay? Bad things really can happen late at night on these streets. What, precisely, are you going to do?'

'That's my own business. That's nothing at all to do with – '

'Now, now,' he interrupted, and she stopped.

'You must not impugn my motives, young lady. You cannot persuade yourself that I mean you any harm. I am simply concerned for you.'

And when I get you into my room I shall place you over my knee, lift up that black skirt that clings to you, and damn well smack your nice round buttocks –

The Irish girl saw something of the sort in his face, and took a step backwards. The move infuriated him, and he was aware of his fingers bunching themselves into both his palms.

'Furthermore,' he said, in a spasm of contempt, 'I don't suppose you've had your supper, have you? Your *chips*. Your *tomato sauce*.'

Her bracelets clashed and jingled as she spun around and walked fast away, sure now of what he was. He stayed where he was, the inexplicable anger leaving him, and he watched the shine go off her hair as she moved on, in a hurry, beyond the immediate splash of the lamp above.

'Don't,' he said. 'Oh, don't. Please!' But she could not hear.

He knew that he had said the wrong things and thought the wrong thoughts, and a sadness drooped over him as he acknowledged his lack of practice. But he had to find someone soon. It was not possible to endure this bewilderment and sense of loss for much longer. And, oh, her hair, and the jump of light into her eyes!

Anger mounted in him again.

'There's no call to be quite so damnably rude, is there, you bog-bound bitch,' he said evenly as he came up in loping strides alongside her, and continued walking, going fast on ahead of her. He heard a soft gasp, and sensed that she had stopped, but he did not turn, his feet slapping hard down on the pavement.

He knew that the weight of his shoes, and their solid clump-a-thump-clump on the hard stone, was stopping him from soaring away from the dirty street and the dirty people who prowled about it.

A young black woman with rose-red lips dabbed her eyes on him in the flash of an automatic routine, but he ignored her, still simmering with the injustice and squalor of things. He stared straight ahead at the diminishing line of darkened buildings, digging his feet down hard. It occurred to him to try a whistle, and cast off this dull and heavy affliction. Perhaps he should jingle the coins in his pocket: no, that would trap his hands in cloth, and he might need them to control his flight, if flight there were once more to be.

He did his best to summon up a simple little tune. 'Poor Mary lies a-weeping'? No. 'Pop goes the weasel'? No, no. 'Who killed Cock Robin' – ?

The grief smacked into him with one swift bounce off the paving slabs. The force of it pushed sockets into his face, dragged at the bone of his knees, and gathered in heavy drops of pain in the tips of his fingers. He could hardly stop from buckling and shrinking under its impact.

The shoes which had kept him earthbound here on the street were now preventing the plunge downwards into the realms of total darkness. Something inexpressibly hideous was trying to suck him down into and through the stones, and on and on past the rumble of the underground train, below the fat worms and slime-packed slugs, deeper than the glistening sewers with their floating lumps of ordure and scrabbling hunch-backed rats, and down to the evil kingdom of the real monsters, all seated around a table so clean and so polite, but dribbling with the venom and the pus of their true natures.

He locked his legs and held fast as scraps of conversation whipped past him, chink of cup on saucer, soft smack of lips on glass, the click and snap of teeth. This is the place where they feed on your innards, and laugh and smile as they tear and bite and chew.

'But they are beautiful. I mean, they really are wonderful,' broke clear, like a clock chime. 'You feel you could pick them off the cards he has done them on, pick them and smell them. I wish you'd let them see, John. Why don't you, John?'

What are they talking about? It didn't matter. The words were falling away, and so were the other sounds. He could more clearly see, again, the outlines of the buildings against the subdued ochreous glow of a city sky at night. There was no need to sink down and down below the thoroughfares of stone and shadow.

A sudden rattle of noise and the stink of stale beer swung out towards him from the opening door of a big gloomy pub. *Esta na estrada errada!* someone shouted. The city was speaking in strange tongues, at almost every corner.

He crossed the street to avoid the open pub door, and the gaggle of exiting foreigners. But to do so he had to step around an already slicked torpedo of dog shit on the edge of the gutter. A warning spurt of nausea from an empty stomach told him to look away, but as he did so the soiled pavement seemed to fuse into a stretch of white tablecloth, a set of faces, a kiss of air from inside his own throat, and then he was free. All at once, he was up and away, leaving his shoes behind him, flying for dear life.

Half a pound of tuppenny rice – skimming now across the slope of the roofing slates, noticing how pitted and pocked they were in the tilt of their slide towards the pavement he had abandoned – *Half a pound of treacle* – over the brown rows of redundant chimney pots, across the flueless towers, and the struts of concrete cladding, into the low billows of dark cloud which turned out to be salmon-pink on the top side. Miles and miles to the stars above, the nursery tune tinkling, and his nostrils quivering a little in the rush of sweeter and sweeter air. *That's the way the money goes. Pop! goes the . . .*

Not with a bump this time, and the jolt at the back of the eyes. Nor had he landed in his waiting shoes – not if these were the ones side by side on the pavement, turning out slightly with the velocity of his departure, the toes screwed away from the dog slick at the edge of the gutter.

His flight had taken him through the night skies, as soft as smoke, and deeper into something less yielding, which became greener and greener and more and more solid. The stuff was pushing itself back against him, with the consciousness of its own life, and so rapidly slowing him as he tumbled and spun in the shock of descent that he was able to mark the change in both colour and texture, and then steady himself into a halt within the whorls of an unexpected and pale purple.

It was not easy to distinguish with the necessary accuracy where the paleness began to get richer until it was now, here within the concave of the upper lip of the bloom, a definite mauve. There was such a small area in which to work, each head veined with white, and clustering close in with the others to make a spike shape at the top of the stem. Accuracy was not enough: you had to be the flower, you had to get inside it, and by intense concentration transfer it into another medium.

John pinched the bridge of his nose, conscious of an extreme weariness, and then frowned at the change of light in the room. A moment ago, surely, the window had been blazing on the far wall, and the uprooted woundwort in the tray had seemed to stretch itself up to meet the radiance of it.

He had felt himself to be, at that instant, fully inside the marsh weed, entering through the toothed leaves. But now the window had scudded towards grey, and the woundwort was showing how desperately it needed the ooze of the ditch where he had captured it.

Instead of clicking on and angling his work lamp, John put down his brush. His eyes were gritty, smarting with the hours of concentration, and the small of his back ached from the bending. Better, then, to straighten up, and use the pencil he kept sharp beside him on the bench.

Stachys palustris, he wrote, on the index card.

He sucked at the blunt end of his pencil, so lost in thought that his eyes went towards the same grey as the window-pane. An irritating little tune from childhood days kept tinkling in his head. He squashed it, then started to write on the card again. The spiky letters were so firmly inscribed that they almost broke through to the other side.

'Hastens the healing of torn flesh.'

The full-stop made a hole. He lifted the pencil, considered awhile, the colour coming back into his eyes. About to add something else, he decided not to, and let the pencil drop with a clatter on to the bench.

'Oh, Christ,' he said, without knowing why.

He did not hear the nervous tap-tap on the door, and did not turn as it opened. Helen stood in the doorway, looking across at him, uneasily. She was determined, this time, to have it out with him, if there was time. But –

'You have to get ready,' she said.

He got up, slowly, and began to walk across to her, with an unusual and even alarming deliberation.

'You said you wanted to get the train,' she said, ready to take a step backwards.

'I said what?' he said, uninflected, and stopped, barely inches away, his face thrust close at her. She feared that he was going to hiss something abominable at her, from between his teeth. But he suddenly dropped his eyes, and the poison went out of them.

'Oh, the train,' he said, apparently exhausted. 'The bloody train.'

'You're showing them your illustrations,' she said, making it sound like an instruction.

'Am I?' He lifted one brow only, as though the other side of his face was too tired and too stiff.

'The publisher,' she said, feeling silly. And then, in a rush: 'What have I done? What is it that makes you talk to me like this?'

'Like what?'

'As though you hate me.'

He studied her. The anxiety speckling her eyes, the sculpt of her lips, the long line of her neck, and the curve below.

'I'd like – ' he began, and stopped.

'Yes?'

'I would have liked to talk,' he said. 'I know you think there's something wrong. I know things went very badly at the dinner last night. I'd like to talk about it, but – there isn't time.'

He finished abruptly, biting off the words, and walked around her, into the tiled passage beyond. She heard him call back as his feet sounded more heavily than usual on the tiles.

'I've got to fly,' he said, over his shoulder.

It was not only the way he had so unceremoniously brushed past her, nor even the change in his tone which bothered her when she awoke in the night, but the strange threat in his laugh as the far door in the passage opened and closed with a dull thud, leaving her alone with a collection of weeds and a room as bright as heaven.

13

It was so fast a descent that his waiting shoes hurt him as he came down into them at full swoop, turning hard on his heel in the same movement, and facing a long and straight avenue where the traffic raced.

How long did he have to walk these streets?

He had fallen in behind a young woman in a flowery dress, who was walking towards the Edgware Road at the far end of the avenue. She was right at the edge of the pavement, her head turned towards the traffic.

A yellow car low on its springs gave a small peep! and slowed to a near stop in front of her. She quickened her stride, and then leaned into the window.

He waited, and watched. The bend of her seemingly flower-strewn body towards the buttercup-yellow of the car made the hint of a memory catch at his breath, and then his skin prickled. Perhaps she was the one who could turn the key and let him through into the secret or, at least, lost garden.

The girl was talking to a shadow inside the car. She hesitated, and then shook her head, an action which enabled him to see that her hair was long and deliberately crinkled, with tiny beads clinging to it like ladybirds. Her face was as white as a ghost, and she could not have been more than seventeen or eighteen years old.

She straightened, and made a gesture of dismissal, but it was without vigour, as though she were too tired to bear the weight of a lifted arm. An obscure oath was flung into the street from the car window, and the car moved off at speed, with an unnecessary squeal of the rear wheels, in the curious way in which a vehicle can so accurately represent the emotions of the driver.

The girl retreated from the edge of the pavement, and stood still, her eyes flicking.

As he watched her, standing still himself, he was uncomfortably aware that the small muscles at the front of his face were pressing in against the bone, so strong was their contraction. The movement continued on down his body, muscle by muscle, gathering strength until reaching his legs. He felt his feet twitch, and their next move would surely be into the first step of a dance rather than a walk. But he controlled them by bracing his knees and making his teeth meet.

He remembered how startled he had been by the first girl's question: 'Do you want business?' and then how sick inside at her casual offer of 'a fuck, or a suck, or anything else you fancy,' so brutally matter of fact out of the wet gash of her mouth. And when he had spoken to the bewildered-looking Irish girl with the clinking bracelets, was it not because he wanted to help her, or protect her?

'Which one am I?'

The question had lettered itself, but it made no sense to him, and he did not think he could have asked it. But it stayed in front of him. The choice was between corruption and salvation.

Perhaps, said something behind his thoughts, perhaps you are the good one. The timid and polite and quietly spoken one. The little boy who did as he was told. The pale-faced one in the darker part of the room, sitting bolt upright, straining to listen and to understand . . .

What little boy?

He bent under the crush of the question, and as he lowered his head, seeing the cracks in the pavement, trickles of memory came back to him, like the blood warming up in a frozen limb. His head tickled and stung, and threw up the image of a man looking hard at him over the top of his spectacles. A wooden chair creaked, in the middle of the bite and the sting, and he knew with certainty that this was indeed a real memory. The man was his father.

The girl in the flowered dress had noticed him. He had begun to walk slowly towards her, without realizing that his shoes were lifting themselves up and putting themselves down.

Corruption, said his left foot. Salvation, said the other. His father still looking over the top of the glasses, and *Ih ill, Oahnn!* sounding, even though he did not think he had moved.

'Hello,' said the girl, with a hopeful smile.

'Hello,' he said, startled to find himself so close to her.

'Do you want to talk to me?' she asked, and then laughed.

'That's not quite what I had in mind,' he said, and laughed as well, delighted with his own ease, and by the shape of her face as it looked up at him. He found himself able to take hold of her elbow, firm under the thin and clinging material of her dress.

'It's thirty pounds. Inside,' she said, quickly, some of the smile going out of her eyes.

'Oh, I think I can manage that,' he said airily, but then dropped his hand from her arm. 'Inside? What do you mean, inside?'

'Hotel. Not car.'

'A hotel?' he started to frown. 'What sort of hotel?'

'Just along the road, just down there.'

When she spoke this time, she showed her bottom teeth. They were aslant against each other, and they were nearer to brown than to white. Two of them were chipped and broken.

'Your teeth,' he said, surprised.

She closed her mouth tight shut, as the child she had been such a little time ago would have done.

'Oh, you poor little thing,' he said, closing his fingers

around her small wrist, before she had any chance to pull her arm away.

'Let go!' she hissed, jerking at his hand.

'You are so young and so pretty,' he said, not loosening his grip. 'And yet it is obvious that you do not take care of yourself.'

His fingers, circling her wrist, were tight enough to whiten her flesh, and she began to feel afraid.

'Let go, you bastard!' she said, her voice rising.

There were many people passing, and a few of them were staring. It was not likely, though, that any of them would go so far as to offer her any help. His hand was clamped on her like a manacle, but, even worse, his eyes were starting to run with tears.

And then his other arm, flapping at the street, summoned up a cruising taxi, as though by magic.

'You poor little thing,' he was repeating, his voice breaking.

'Mind your own fucking business!' she yelled.

The people who had stopped to look at them were not sure what to do. A worried-looking man came closer, but with his hands half up, palms outward, over-ready to retreat, saying, 'Hey.'

The taxi had pulled in, and the driver was staring out.

'Let go!' the girl was shouting.

'I'm getting her off the streets!' he yelled, at the timidly interfering man, at the taxi-driver, and at the small crowd which was so quickly gathering.

He pulled her towards the taxi, easily overbearing her struggling and her clawing. She was as light as a child. But she was making a noise like one, too, and showing those spoiled bottom teeth again, in a way that infuriated him.

'Not in here,' the taxi-driver called to him. 'Not in my cab!'

'It's my daughter! It's my little girl!' he shouted back. 'I'm getting her off the streets! I've found her! My daughter!'

'No – !' she was screaming, 'No! I'm not – ! No!'

He had wrenched the passenger door open before the driver, momentarily thrown, could lock it. She was bundled in like a plastic doll as her legs splayed and kicked and her bad teeth tried to bite. He did not once let go of her wrist, and plunged headlong into the back of the taxi with her.

'New Cavendish Street,' he bellowed authoritatively at the driver, the first name to come into his head.

'Now listen here – ' the driver began, a flush on his neck and face as he swivelled around to look at them.

'New Cavendish Street,' he repeated. 'At the corner of Great Titchfield Street,' a precise location going plop! in his head.

The girl continued to scream and flounder, writhing herself half off the seat so that only his grip of her wrist kept her off the floor.

'Don't! Don't! Don't!' she was trying to say, over and over, terrified to find herself so swiftly and firmly captive.

The taxi-driver opened his door to get out of the cab, with the quick hunching of the shoulders which shows a man preparing himself for violence. He was thus unable to see the blow which knocked the thin girl into silence, the free hand used like a hammer, crashing down on top of her head.

The punch stunned her, and her shoulders went slack, though her eyes stayed open.

'It's all right, driver. Everything is in order now. A family crisis.'

The driver looked at the limply submissive girl and then at the man. She was quiet, and he looked respectable enough. It was not the driver's affair. He flicked off his For Hire light, and drove away, leaving a small crowd on the pavement. They looked disappointed.

In the cab, the girl half surfaced, but feeling as though the thinnest bones at the top of her skull had been crushed.

'No,' she whispered, no fight in her, 'don't.'

He stroked the back of her hand with the tips of his fingers.

'Don't be frightened, little one,' he said, quietly.

'No,' she whispered again. 'No. Please.'

He smiled and shook his head and patted her arm. 'I hope I didn't hurt you too much, you poor little thing,' he said, close to her ear. The small, soft lobe fascinated him, and he had to pull his face back a little to prevent his tongue flicking out and licking it.

'I abhor and detest violence,' he said, more severely, 'but you were out of control, my dear. The noise you were making. And your language – well! If I hear any more of it, I shall have to wash out your pretty little mouth with soap and water. Do you understand me? Do you follow what I am saying to you?'

She did not seem able to answer, but stared at him, her eyes on his mouth, as though trying to make sense of what was being said. A drawing on the page, she was, above the italicized caption. *She stared at him fearfully, her eyes like saucers in her small white face.*

Some old magazine, he thought to himself, suddenly queasy, or a boy's book, something I must have read in the past. Perhaps in that very same room in which he had been told to sit still. Half in the window of the cab, and half in the street glimmers outside, the eyes stared in at him, over the top of the spectacles.

'I don't want you to think of me as an unreasonable person,' he said to the cowering girl, the words a thrill on his skin and a tansy-taste in his mouth. 'I want you to ask yourself whether it is fair, whether it is just. Wouldn't you say so? Mmm?'

Again, she did not seem able to answer, even though he said, 'Mmm?' once more, and then, 'Mmmm?' with a longer hum.

The taxi-driver was keeping as much of an eye on his

99

interior mirror as on the street ahead. So far, he could see nothing especially amiss, but his instinct kept him alert. Day in, day out, the great grey city was filling up above the bilge line with lunatics, thieves and morons, and he never knew when any one of them could be sitting a couple of feet and a fold of glass behind him . . .

What a little tart, though. What a bleeding scrubber.

'Please,' she said, still saucer-eyed. 'Don't hurt me.'

'I don't want to hurt a hair on your head,' he said, sounding incredulous, and even indignant. 'I have absolutely no intention of harming you. I have been looking for you for a long time, and there's a great deal I want to talk to you about, and – oh, you poor little creature! Please! Don't tremble like this! I promise you faithfully, no harm will come to you at *my* hands. Trust me. Believe in me!'

She had a bad headache now, and was already exhausted, but she tried a little smile, making sure not to show her bottom teeth.

'That's better,' he said, with a sigh, and let go of her wrist for the first time since dragging her off the pavement. 'I dislike fuss and noise, especially when there is no need for it.'

'Where – where are you taking me – ?'

He had to lean his face closer to her, hardly able to hear. As he did, his tongue flicked out and then back in again, prevented once more from licking at the lobe of her ear or the soft line of her young neck.

'What are you going to do?' she asked, in a whimper.

She was so terribly frightened that she could not remember what her friend had said, about what to do when you were stupid enough to land yourself with a nutter.

'I don't know. I'm not sure,' he said, frowning.

His uncertainty gave her back a little courage, and her voice was stronger when she asked him again where he was taking her.

'I don't know. I'm not sure,' he repeated.

He turned his head away, as quickly as though it were mounted on a spring, to look out of the window on his side of the cab. They were passing a video shop which had Arabic lettering on stickers splashed across the glass door, and a poster display showing, many times over, a man with a scar on his cheek leaning close over the back-tilting head of a young woman, her hair hanging free, and her eyes and her mouth set for screaming.

That's me, he thought. Oh God, that could be me.

'The least I can do, in the circumstances,' he said, whipping his head back to her as swiftly as he had turned away, 'is to give you some money. That's only right and proper.'

'Money?'

The girl had been moving her hand, cautiously, towards the lever in her door, ready to make a leap for freedom as soon as the taxi stopped for the traffic lights, or even slowed to make a turn.

'Money,' he nodded. 'And much more than you asked for.'

She was momentarily tempted to drop her covertly stretching hand, which he had not appeared to notice.

'Yeah?' she asked, a mere quiver of a word.

'Take your hand away from the door!'

The blade of his stare, and the hardness in his tone, made her obey at once. The top of her head was throbbing fiercely from his blow, and she did not want another. Besides, she felt so wretchedly tired, and the pills seemed to be rattling about behind her eyes. Threads of light were flashing and coiling at the edge of her sight, but they were calming themselves into slow, luminous bubbles of an electric blue.

When the taxi pulled up with a jolt at the traffic lights he looked sharply across at her again, but saw that she had fallen asleep, slumped into her small frame.

He studied her, and his expression softened. She looked so fragile, with such daintily made bones and so little flesh, except at her small breasts which pushed against her flowered dress. 'Like peaches,' he thought, and his throat went dry.

There was a premature furrow in her forehead, and a thin thread of a line made an almost perfect circle around her neck, like a necklace. He could see the faint glisten of the down that she had not yet lost on her cheeks, under the badly applied, caked make-up. Her eyelids, closed now, had been plastered with dark blue, almost black, and some of it had clogged on the long lashes.

Once more, he could sense the grief about to break inside himself, from somewhere deeper than he could reach, the part of his mind which knew about his past life.

He did not know what he was doing in this smelly and lurching vehicle. The sadness was coming up his throat, now, and into his nose and his eyes, so he took hold of her hand in order not to be alone. The clench of her fingers had to be uncurled, but she did not stir. Her hand was small and cold within his.

'I'll watch over you,' he said. 'I'll take care of you.'

She showed no sign of having heard, and he wondered whether to shake her back into life, so that he could tell her these things.

'Lick her face,' said a voice he had forgotten.

'No, no,' he murmured, to himself.

'Flick your tongue over her sweet little face. Go on!' urged the man he realized was his secret friend, grown now, and come back to him. 'Flick your tongue over her eyelids, and along the line of her cheekbone, and then slide the tip of it between her lips. Go on. Do it!'

'Oh, no,' he moaned. 'No, no. Mustn't do that. Must not.'

At first, there was the taste of something stale and powdery and perfumed, but the rasp of his tongue soon went below that to the softness of her flesh, and then the full swell of her lips.

She did not stir, not even as his tongue pushed her mouth

sufficiently open to slide inside. When it touched her teeth, he pulled his head back quickly, and wiped his hand across his mouth.

'No,' he said, out loud. 'Oh, no.'

'Put your hand on her sweet little breast. Go on!'

She still did not move or open her eyes when his fingers found her nipple, which was easily accessible. Nor did she wake when the sounds of his weeping grew from a pathetic little mew into a violent sob, strong enough to throw his head off her, and jerk his hand away from the top of her legs.

The cab, too, stopped with a suddenness which caused an affronted hoot from the car behind. The appalled cab-driver, mirror-watching, had had enough.

'What's going on?' he said, as he wrenched open the passenger door on the pavement side. 'What the bloody hell do you think you're doing in my cab?'

The girl looked as though she had passed out, or perhaps even worse. And the man was clenched up, his knees bumping against his eyebrows, making a disgusting howling noise.

'For Christ's sake!' he said, angry and embarrassed, and reached in to grasp at the howling man's arm.

Before he could get a hold, he reared back in shock as the man sprang out at him, in a leap which seemed scarcely possible from a sitting and hunched and weeping position.

The air was knocked out of his lungs as the man hurtled past him. By the time the driver had sucked in another breath, the cab door was swinging loose, and the sobbing man was already beyond the glowing back lights of the taxi, arms driving like pistons, shoes slap, slap, slapping on first the pavement and then the road, a shadow elongating, shrinking and then stretching as he went under a pendulous street lamp.

'Hey! You!' the driver called, in a shocked reflex, but meaninglessly.

'Run!' said John, the taste of blood in his mouth.

'Run! Run!' gasped his secret friend, the other John.

They were soon out of sight, swerving in the way soldiers do to avoid a sniper's line of fire, the one dragging in his breath in rasping sobs, and the other blowing it out in a frantic whistling sound, pant pant pant, with hard pounding feet, faster and faster, until there was no need to touch the pavement at all.

14

Helen was glad that she once again had some time to call her own. For too long, from spring into summer and now the drawing in before the fall, his stooped and brooding presence in the room with the plants, hour after hour, had made her increasingly anxious and, finally, definitely afraid. She had watched a man gradually lose what had been an habitual, unflustered geniality as easy and as comfortable as the old corduroys he liked to wear at the weekends, and replace it with silence, or moroseness, and an inexplicable hostility.

It was possible that the change in him had been triggered by the loss of his job, but she could not believe that there was not also something else going on in him. Something to do with her.

This space while he went to London gave her the chance to ponder through to what it might be. But not yet, not for a moment. She knew how quickly she could make herself feel guilty. Their agreement not to speak about her life before meeting him had turned into a device, for her, for blocking that past out of her mind as completely as though it had never been. If she thought of it at all, it was as an invention, a pretence. His invention, his pretence. His.

She constructed for herself various scenes within the offices of the publisher John had gone to town to see. One of those interchangeable young men of high education and low market value who perch for a while in the boughs of publishing houses like young crows. Letting out modulated caw-caws and learning how to riffle their feathers a little before flitting off to other nests and potentially more nourishing carrion in other fields.

But *this* one would be so impressed with John's work that he would make everything all right again. A magician was needed, to wave his wand and restore life to what it had been only a few months ago.

She saw the previously polite and yet slightly condescending face of the publisher being transformed by surprise and then overtaken by respect and enthusiasm: 'But these are – oh, these are absolutely wonderful. They are breathtaking!'

Wild clary or yellow rattle or that complicated thing called bugle, each glowing on its small white card, already the shape and size of the page. The white in a leaf or a flower was not simply the unpainted white of the card, however, which was so often the cheapskate way of flower books. Everything John had painted was as fresh as the dawn.

'Oh, no, no,' the man would say to John's half-apologetic, slow smile of a question, 'you might think that there's only a limited market for this sort of thing, but, believe me, you'd be wrong! Think of *The Country Diary of an Edwardian Lady*. Think of *The Frampton Flora*. Oh, there's a market all right.'

Railway bookstalls. Country newsagents. Book clubs. Special editions for schools. Licences for birthday and greetings cards. Shopping-bag designs.

'I would even go so far as to say that a book of the kind you propose, with full-plate illustrations of such a startling quality as these . . .'

What would not be going too far to say? An old avarice gleamed, briefly. Spin-offs. New commissions. Chat-show and even grander radio and television appearances as John orchestrated, so to speak, a big resurgence of interest in Our Native Heritage, the wild flowers of the roadside and wasteground, pretty little heads stirring to an unaccustomed attention.

Even after she had more sensibly readjusted the face and

the words and cut back the foliated excess with severe clippers, enough of the root remained to sprout again, in her mind. After all, she had seen the paintings for herself. She knew how vivid they were. Never mind the strange words on the index-cards. Forget the scrawled KILL PENNY. Forget the way he had looked at her yesterday morning before leaving for the train.

She looked at the clock. Ten minutes to four. Ten minutes, and he would be in the Covent Garden office, opening out the portfolio, and (please, God) re-establishing his connections with the outside world, the working world. Then she would be able to see whether it was the snapping of that link which had so badly upset his own sense of himself, and therefore of her, too.

She looked at the clock.

The second glance, an unnecessary duplicate, made her see herself as another might. She had not until then realized that she was standing in the middle of the sitting-room. She had not seen that her hands were folding and unfolding, and that her muscles were so tight, her shoulders so stiff, and her jaw so clenched. Anyone observing her from the window would know that she was threaded with stress and –

And then, with a jump inside, she sensed that she *was* being observed. KILL PENNY leapt at her, the pencil marks deeply inscribed, as though on the back of her eyelids.

Helen turned, with a catch in her breath, to look swift and sidelong at the window, and she jumped inside again.

A dark, hunched-up figure had flitted past the pane. Or was it a shadow? 'A shadow,' she said, hearing her heart beat faster and faster. 'A shadow. It's a shadow.' It was that sort of day in that sort of September, where the sky was mostly in flux and all its promises inconstant. Every afternoon the shadows danced and then they were driven away again.

In any case, it made no sense for there to be someone at the window, peeping into the room. It was a garden window, with an oval of flowerbeds directly beneath, and the twisting arm of an old, mostly unproductive apple tree wavering a witch's way across the upper third of the glass.

'A shadow. A shadow. It was a shadow.'

But if someone *had* been standing there, it followed that they could be up to no good.

Mr Milne, the jobbing Scot who helped in the garden, had gone home to the village several hours ago. Today was not the day for the cleaning lady. Nobody else was expected. And even if they were, that was not the place to stand . . .

The branch of the apple tree often behaved badly on windy nights, paying back for its neglect by clawing and tapping against the glass. It could be playing its old melodrama once more. Except, there was not enough wind to move the branches as much as that.

Helen informed herself, would-be decisively, that it was illogical to be nervous. The house might not be blessed with the sunniest of dispositions, and the Victorian master who had built it out of the local stone must sometimes have had a frown beneath his top hat and whiskers. But it was a safe dwelling in a calm part of the land, on a small rise off a little-used road which could more accurately be called a lane. The village beyond it, in the fold of farmland, had escaped new road building, and nothing bad, little new, ever happened here. The contrast with her life before her marriage was about as complete as it could be: peace, monogamy, polite conversation, and little triangles of bread and butter for tea.

The most sensible thing, of course, was to go outside into the garden and look around. But then she imagined the sound of her feet on the gravel path, and the big tealeaf tree murmuring, and the slight chill of light as it refracted on the surface of the pond.

Instead of going out, she tilted her head to listen.

Everything was quiet. She let the silence come into her, and combed through it. There was an unease out there, a hush of tension, a sense of the waiting in things, like the trees, the flowers, the bits of gravel, and the sky looking at itself in the pond. A bird trilled in sudden alarm. And her quickening pulse again went thump-a-bump-bump.

Stop it! Stop it, you fool!

The command she directed at herself was fierce enough to propel her across the room to the window. She stood close enough to it to be able to place her forehead against the glass if she had wanted. The curtain touched her bare arm.

There was nothing to be seen that she did not expect to be out there. A few sad puddles glinted at the edge of the gravel, and the earth was black with moisture. The sky was full of pictures, but she did not bother with those. It was going to rain again.

'No point in going out there, and bringing mud into the house,' she said to herself, not recognizing it as an evasion.

She went out of the room, from the soft give of the carpets to the hard smack of the tiles, her feet suddenly clicking, past the inherited, throaty clock in the hall, and bolted the back door.

As she turned back, feeling more sure of herself, she stopped and wrinkled her nose. The faint smell she had detected in the room where John worked had found its way into the hall. Sniffing the air, Helen could again detect a tinge of an animal odour in it, sick, alien, elusive, and threatening.

Tick-h tock-h tick-h tock-h.

'Jesus Christ, stop it!' she said out loud, and slammed her way back into the sitting-room, where she clicked on the lamps at least an hour before they were needed. The light sheened at the angle of a picture frame, and she thought she saw a shape form itself and then dissolve in the corner of the painting.

'It's catching, this,' she said, again out loud, and with a simulated hah! of indignation.

Since the earth in the flowerbeds is so damp and sticky, a

thought said before she banished it, then the obvious means of knowing whether anyone had been snooping at the window was to check and see if footprints had been left.

'A cloven hoof,' shouted a banished thought as it was forced into retreat, and she settled herself down with a bite of the lower lip and the infra-red control pad to watch the children's programmes on television.

The bright colours and gaudy music of an animated cartoon swirled up on the screen, and a narrator told a tale in a fruity voice-over which had achieved its greatest renown in commending jam tarts and chocolate sponges.

'Tap-tap, said the bent old apple tree at the window-pane – ' the narrator said, with an avuncular chuckle.

This was too much of a coincidence to be comfortable, or even entirely plausible.

She used the remote-control panel to change the picture, and as her neck went cold, wished she could as easily transport herself into another scene.

15

John lay flat out and fully clothed on top of his bed in the hotel room. He was staring up at the white ceiling in an attempt to make his mind steady into and then fix upon any one sequence of genuinely consecutive thought, in the same way that a giddy man might try to find one stable image in the flux and the whirl.

His head was full of skeetering puzzles and disconnected pictures, and he could not tell which of them belonged to his own past, or which ones might be more important than the others. A room in a comfortable old house, a ticking clock, a pair of eyes over the top of heavily framed spectacles, a purple flower, a woman's head on a pillow, her hair spreading like a fan, the pebbles splashing into a pond, and a horse cropping the grass with the thickening sky falling on to its back.

It felt like the moments immediately leading into a deep sleep, when dreams reach forward and make a premature claim to their territory. But he was no longer so tired, and he knew he had not closed his eyes. Besides, he could hear the sounds of the hotel, and the noises of the traffic in the street below, none of which had the resonances of a dream.

In the distance, he heard a man laugh too loudly in the long corridor, and then a door close too firmly. The elevator tinkled as it came to his floor, hissed open and shut, and tinkled again on its way up or down. A far-off radio sent out a dull bass throb of the kind which makes every other piece of modern popular music sound as though it were written by the same retarded composer. Boom-boom-boom.

What, he wondered, can be the significance of these things?

'Nothing. No significance,' said a voice he now recognized. 'You're on your own. You are free. You can do anything. And everything you ever wanted to do.'

'Our Father which art in – ' John began, in fear.

'Don't!' said his friend with a contemptuous hiss.

And John, on the hotel bed, remembered another bed in another room, with a steep slope to its ceiling, and Our Lord Jesus Christ fading back into a distant boom from downstairs.

Boom-boom-boom went the radio, somewhere along the corridor.

John could feel his mind coming back towards him. Inch by inch, the immediate past edged into view.

He was on a train. It was *the* train. Why? He knew there was something extremely important that he was supposed to do. Why wouldn't it come back to him? Clues were everywhere. There were too many of them, including the laugh outside in the corridor, the slam of the door, the tinkle of the elevator, the noise of the radio.

Meaning fell in folds at the window, lay in tufts on the floor, traced its messages in the patterns on the wall, and repeated itself in the sounds from the street below. But how could he decipher it? Why was it signalling at him with such urgency?

Once more, with his teeth meeting, he mauled over what had come back to him. A woman by a pond, with a faceless infant: but that was the remnant of a dream, and might not count. But the same woman, perhaps, had walked down a hotel corridor and tapped with the crook of her long fingers on the door. The same woman, too, who had looked up at him when she was doing something unbelievably disgusting.

'Kill Penny,' he said, and then frowned, for the words had no meaning.

112

He thought instead of the man looking over his glasses at the little boy who was once himself. This, in turn, brought back to him the recollection of a breathless descent into the tendrils of a plant, and the seep of mauve which came from its bloom. A flowering, at the same time, of a room with a wooden bench, the dig of a pencil, a smell of . . .

A smell that he knew he knew, but could not make real. A man hunched over, eyes stinging, head aching with the effort of concentration. A despair. The smell was the stink of despair.

'Kill Penny,' he said again, out loud, and then went quiet.

The mauve petals drew his thoughts once more, after he had brooded a while about the mysterious and repellent injunction. Flowers were clearly of importance in his past. The man hunched over the bench, and the man looking over the top of his glasses were not the same, and yet they were the same. The two rooms were different. The one with the bench was bright with light, and the other had pools of darkness. Flowers joined them in some way.

He squinted down the length of his body at his shoes, still on his feet. Where had they been taking him? Why had he been running, with someone shouting out into the night, behind him? A flush warmed his cheek, and he knew it as shame.

Suddenly, the angle of his shoes made him think of the hands of a clock. He automatically looked at his wrist.

Ten minutes to four in the afternoon.

There is something important I am supposed to do.

The feeling was so strong that it made him sit up on the bed. And then, because it would not relent, he was forced to walk up and down on the floor, going from the bed to the window and back to the bed again. He had a fleeting impression that he had paced in a bedroom in exactly this manner on some other occasion, but where or when remained a mystery.

Elsewhere called so strongly that this time he had no sensation of flight at all. The carpet at his feet threw him off with no more than a shake of its synthetic tufts, stain resistant, and he landed in equally soft but rather sticky mounds of dark earth, which were banked up around tall flowers with luminous shell-like heads, beneath a gnarled tree. The window in front of him looked at first sight to be made of obsidian, but then he saw that it was darkly reflecting back a small part of the sky.

By moving his head, he could drive off the bits of heavily drooping cloud and the reflected glimmer of lead in between. The room behind the window-pane quivered into view, although the chairs and the walls were partly subverted by the heads of the tallest of the flowers and the overhang of the tree. The sky itself floated in the room, and then drifted off a little into an opaque gloom as he stepped, very cautiously closer.

A slender woman with long hair was standing in the middle of the room, her back to the window. His chest began to burn with pain at the sight of her, and his eyes quickly filled, refracting her into the droplets of a rainbow. He blinked rapidly until the image of her became clearer again.

Although she was turned away from him, he had a glimpse of her hands, which were folding and unfolding. Her shoulders were stiff, and he recognized the tension and anxiety from his recent observations of his own limbs.

'Never mind, oh, never mind,' he said under his breath, lips almost touching the glass, 'don't fret so, little one.'

He tried to follow the direction of her gaze, and realized that she was looking at the carriage-clock on the mantel. The hands on the oblong face were difficult to discern, as part of the sky and the branch of the tree superimposed themselves in between, but he made out, all at once, that they were pointing ten minutes to four o'clock.

The woman looked around, suddenly, and as though

frightened. It was such a shock to him to see that her face was a whore's face that he was back on the tufted carpet in his hotel room before he had time to screw up his mouth and spit on to the window-pane.

Up and down, up and down he went, from the window to the bed and the bed to the bathroom door, simmering with anger and contempt. But, gradually, the after-image of the silvery hands on the clock replaced the woman's soiled countenance. Ten minutes to four. There is something important that he must do.

The time. It had to do with the time.

He stopped his pacing and put every last vestige of energy into his thoughts. An appointment, the signals were saying. The sounds along the corridor and the noises in the street all agreed. *You have an appointment.*

Four o'clock! Tick-a-tick-a-tick. It was more important that he get out of the room than try to find the reason. His shoes might take him to wherever it was he was supposed to be. The tick-a-tick-a-tick feeling, a rapid clock, was now so much of an imperative that he had no doubt that he must leave at once.

He hurriedly straightened his tie, letting the tight knot press into his throat. His hair was smoothed down by his palms, and at the same time he ran his tongue across the front of his teeth. There was a sour taste in his mouth, and he wondered if it was his feet that he could smell, the socks clinging and damp at the heel and toes.

Too late to do anything about it, he thought, in a rush of panic, the tick-a-tick-a-tick racing, as he slammed his way out of the room, and skidded on the corridor floor in his haste to reach the metallic ting! of the lifts.

A tweedy woman with an upsweep of silver hair was carrying an unkempt, toy-sized dog under her arm, and she pressed the button as he came running towards her.

'I've pressed it several times. It's so slow,' she said, and then her eyes widened and she stepped quickly backwards. The little dog snarled, and started to yap.

The tick-a-tick-a-tick was so demanding that he did not even realize that his expression had frightened the old woman and her toy animal. He rattled at the lattice in front of the elevator shaft, shouting for the cage to come. The woman had already decided to use the stairs.

When he eventually reached the pavement outside the hotel, he was in such a fluster and a flurry that he did not at first comprehend that his shoes had greeted the street like a flinty old friend. They strode off, heel and toe, clack and thump, knowing what to do.

He allowed them to go where they would. It was a question of handing over now, for he found that he could no longer think of what to do. He did not even interfere when his shoes took him almost directly into the path of a careering red bus, packed with passengers. Startled faces stared at him from the windows, and the air whipped up by the bus was close enough to make his eyelashes flicker.

A car hooted at him, and then another, and someone yelled before he reached the far pavement, which was not as safe as he might have supposed, were he thinking at all of the urban perils. He could not understand why a metal waste-bin, strapped to a lamp-post, should nudge him so viciously in the hip. A discarded cigarette packet with a red V on it like an adder's tongue flew up at him, threateningly. A pigeon did the same in a fat grey flutter.

He kept going, but in such a rush that he staggered on the crowded stone steps that descended to the Underground ticket office, and several people glared or muttered, in a hurry themselves. The growing rumble of an approaching train, somewhere below, seemed to be the noise in a thousand protesting throats.

A press of bodies warned of the immediately coming rush-hour, and he found it difficult not to get himself mixed up in their busy arms and legs. Afternoon rain had left its damp cling on too many of the clothes, and he could smell the different kinds of cloth and plastic and rubber. Wet on the hair coaxed out the odour of scalps beneath, and there was a mixture of follicle grease and hairspray to drift up to his nose.

He wrinkled his nostrils, but it was no good. All the varieties of stench which the human body generated wafted towards him. Sticky, foul, acidic, mixed with powder and paste and stale food, flying on droplets of mucus, dribbles of snot, goblets of saliva, hundreds upon thousands of microbes, pullulating layers of bacteria, dead skin cells, ear wax and pimple secretion.

Voices yapped and burbled incontinently, hands grappled, shoulders lurched and pushed, eyes jabbed and darted, feet scraped. He was in a queue, which was bending in on itself, and moving forward too slowly.

'You can't use one of those so-called mice on a smooth surface,' the man in front was saying. 'And what the heck, if you have to have a special surface, why not go for a digitizing tablet instead, eh?'

Tick-a-tick-a-tick, coming through the incomprehensible blur of words.

'Come on, come on, come on,' he said between his teeth, keeping his elbows pressed tight in against his sides.

'I think you shouldn't talk down the tracker ball. Better than a joystick. And they don't trap the dirt.'

Dirt? Dirt? The disgust was overwhelming him, and in order to stop it drowning the last few cells in his throat and lungs he pushed out hard with the flat of both his hands, his elbows still tucked. The stocky little man in front, midway into a sentence about computers, shot forward under the impact, colliding awkwardly with a woman carrying a folded umbrella.

The stocky man made a startled noise, and the woman a hurt one.

117

'Come, come on, come on!' John repeated, but no more loudly.

He sensed that the man in front of him, the listener in the interrupted conversation, had urine stains on his underwear. One reluctant, half-stifled gulp of air, and it could be picked up, sharp and sour within all the other smells. The woman, too, with the flushed, indignant gobble-gobble of a stare, bending to pick up the umbrella she seemed to have thrown to the floor. Old talcum powder between the deep creases of her pouched skin, and a tiny gelatinous blob of white stuff not sufficiently hidden in the corner of one of her eyes.

'Filth,' he said, presuming it to be for his ears alone, and pushing out with his hands again, not in order to touch, but to avoid being touched.

The stocky man cannoned forward again. He had to grab in a desperate scramble at the wrong parts of several others to stop himself crashing down into a heap upon the concrete floor.

'What?' John asked, with a blink, and a certain alarm, as many more angry faces and abusive mouths turned upon him. They looked out of control, guard dogs off their leashes. It was exactly how he had always dreaded it would be.

'Bloody maniac!' said someone, jabbing at him with unclean hands, a small fleck of scum at the edge of his lips.

'What? What – ?' he asked, trying to clamp his arms even more tightly to his sides, anxious to touch as few of these stinking beasts as possible.

'What do you think you're doing?'

'I'm afraid I am in somewhat of a hurry,' he explained, putting up the flimsy barrier of his own formality.

He wondered why the woman who had dropped and picked up her umbrella was now herself spreadeagled on the concrete, her legs apart in such an unseemly fashion, showing a frill of something sadly lavender near the top of her ridged and marbled thighs. And why was she making so much noise? Her mouth hanging open like that.

Elsewhere, said his mind, as the scuffle around him increased, and a fist thudded into his shoulder, *elsewhere!*, and the woman yelping on the floor, and – oh, soar, go free, fly! –

A soft landing. Furniture and walls through the glass again, with wisps of sky and cloud about them.

'"Tap, tap," said the bent old apple tree at the window pane . . .'

It was an electronic voice, muffled by the closed window, and instantly changing to what he recognized as a sales pitch. At the edge of his vision, contained in the glowing box within the room, a woman was tilting back her head to suck and then bite at a confectionery bar. He knew what *that* was, too. The chocolate flashed and revolved on the screen, quickly wiped away, or swallowed by the next thing to be sold. A tub of fat, coming out of buttercups and daisies. It was oddly familiar: these bouncy jingles, emphatic claims and grinning trust-me mouths must have had some connection with his life. A bad one. A dangerous one.

He shifted his feet in the damp earth, and put his hand on the apple tree in order to have the touch of something real against his skin. He wondered why pictures so obviously packed with lies were being beamed into an empty room.

The room itself was an ache of unrealistic happiness. The disposition of the comfortable armchairs, the slight cross-angle of the plumpy and gaily cushioned sofa, the pictures on the walls, and the quiet glint of the bevelled carriage-clock on the mantel, all these things had the quality of a genuine memory and not a dream. They reassured, and seemed to smile back at him, amiable in the way they fitted together, with no sharp edges, no cries, and no whimpers. If he smashed his way through the glass he would find a refuge.

Home. The word beckoned, and warmed. 'Home.' He tried

it, speaking out loud. The soft breathing sound of its beginning, becoming round and full like a ripe fruit, and then closing, not with a thrust of a tongue or a brutal click of the teeth, but in the warmth of meeting lips, unhurried against each other.

But before he had time to savour the word again, and decide whether to break the separating glass, he had to bob back quickly as the empty room took on unexpected life. The back and the wings of an armchair sprouted a head of long hair, which detached itself, and became a standing woman.

'Penny,' he said, in a jag of hurt.

She looked at the window, with a frown. He kept himself out of sight, behind the twisted and knobbed tree, and clung to it, getting a dusty green powder on his hands from the elderly bark, as he tried to stay where he was. But his feet were not quite so deep in the wet soil as they had been a moment ago, and he could feel his body being pulled away again. The pain was almost too great to bear as his ligaments stretched and stretched until they threatened to snap, exposing the vivid nerve to the screaming air.

'Help me. Please help me!' he cried, and clawed at the pane, which was darkening again as the leaden sky demanded all the glass. The room quivered and shimmered for a second, and the woman in it, but then dipped completely out of view as the pain gathered itself from his body and settled into his head.

The bump completed the agony, jarring him from head to toe and all but snapping his neck, landing as he did in a half-circle of hostile people.

The woman on the stone floor was still making peculiar noises as she lay knees up and legs apart in the dirt, and a young man was thrusting a big face of bone at him, exactly as though he intended to butt.

'Get off!' John hissed, pulling his elbows clear so that his hands had more room to strike back.

It is true, then; it really is the case. People can suddenly turn and attack you, showing their teeth. They will spit their venom at you, and breathe all over you, for no apparent reason. You walk up and down in the world amongst them at your peril. At any moment, they will swivel on the balls of their feet, and snap and snarl and rend you, in a stink of hatred.

If only he could have broken through the barrier of glass and its sky reflections, and taken possession of the room he had just seen. He would never leave it. He would take off his shoes and chain down his feet rather than risk flying again into the middle of this fetid madhouse . . .

He bunched his shoulders, flailed out with his fists, put his head down, and bullocked his way through the herd. Several others were knocked reeling as they came down the steps. He stepped on legs and feet and shopping bags, and kept his fists whirling. There were cries of pain and shouts of anger. Hands grappled at him, and plucked at his clothes, clawed at his face.

But he had broken free, and was back on the pavement again, still running, arms pumping and knees coming up high, forcing a path through the throng.

Eventually, he slowed to a walk. He was gasping for breath, and his skin was clammy with sweat. Small, salty globules of it oozed up on his forehead and slid down into his eyes. But at least he was safer now, and no one was trying to hit him.

Through the hum and choke of the endless traffic he could see the trees of the park, heavy with leaves. He had run all the way from the Underground station in Praed Street to the Bayswater Road.

The park shimmered ahead of him like a lost land. There would be grass there, and small flowers, and softer ground for his shoes. Even the air would smell sweeter, for some of the urban stench would be filtered out by the foliage.

But the intransigent sense that he was supposed to be

somewhere, that he had to do a specific thing of enormous import, was tick-a-tick-a-tick in his mind again, now that the sweat was no longer seeping out on to his skin.

His watch showed half past four, and his head said, Late! Late!, and his shoes took matters into their own soles and, without ado, hurtled him across the wide and busy road, forcing him to take no notice of the hoots and the squealing of brakes and the grinding clump as one set of bumpers collided with another.

The stubby grass stretched out before him, yielding easily to his imperious but now apparently solaced feet. It smelt faintly of the afternoon rain, with the hint of an autumn meadow triumphantly persisting. Further in, the ground rose and fell in a more natural fashion, as though preening about its escape from a street cladding, and the disfigurement of drains and gutters.

Everything was better. The people were less thickly bunched together. There were bird trills above the hum of the traffic. He could once again put his hand on the bark of a tree, and feel the ridges of the roots beneath him.

There was a woman in the distance, further into the trees, beside a horse. No, it was a pony. No, a very large and shaggy dog. Perhaps it was the perspective, or the lessening of other distractions, but he could no longer be sure of the precise outline of things.

The boughs above were beginning to lean in towards each other with the suggestion of a snicker, a hint of malice. A leaf fluttered down and lay on a bare patch in the grass.

He stared down at the leaf, struggling with sadness, and then stared up the tree which had cast it off and sent the message. The sky was a battleship grey between the lattice of the branches, and it looked as though it had considerable reserves of melancholy to dump upon him.

Give it up, said the sky. Lie down. There is nothing else you can do.

16

Angela, stopping her sewing-machine of a little, humped French car with a crunch on the gravel, thought that the funny-forbidding old house was sailing off rudderless into the night. A high wind was sweeping in from the stone-walled fields, and the house looked as though it had been blown from its billowing moorings. The trees around it bent and bobbed and whipped at each other, a loose shutter at the outhouse creaked and banged, and the bushes at the edge of the drive were frothing white as they showed the undersides of their leaves.

No wonder Helen got a bit nervous when she was on her own in this place. 'I wondered if you were doing anything special – ?' she had said to Angela on the telephone, less than an hour before. The tone had put Angela on her guard.

Angela had many secrets, and she was not always sure which box to keep them in, or which lid to lift at which moment. She was always wary when one of the local young married women spoke to her in an 'I wondered if' sort of voice on the telephone.

Helen had sounded like someone trying not to sound strained: in other words, more than usually strained. It was soon evident, though, that the stress was not something that need trouble Angela, and she had agreed to 'come over'.

She observed that there were a lot of lights blazing at the windows of Acre House. These signs of reassurance had, as is often the case, an opposite effect. The house, lit thus, and looming against the windy and darkening sky, made her think of an old thriller she had seen on television the other evening, though there was little about this place which was specifically like the grotesque mansion in the American film. Rather, the big tree at the side of the house was moaning more in the spirit of the three witches in her O-level set-book play.

Angela smiled to and at herself, feeling both educated and vaguely malicious, a common enough combination, as she gave the ornately grimacing iron door-knocker an unnecessarily hefty couple of slaps. That'll make her jump, she thought. Helen was the sort of woman you were never wholly sure you liked or not. There were mysterious currents in her, other lives, other attitudes, and an occasional cool stare that made you feel more than uncomfortable.

Helen did jump. She was expecting Angela, she had heard the car chug-chug through the gate, but she jumped all the same as the knocker banged. She had to stand for a moment in the hall to compose herself, and then went to open the front door. As she felt the tug of the wind against it, and a whistle on the other side, she had to swallow down the swift half-image of a dark and winged shape falling in through the widening gap, its face open in an awful scream.

'Hoo, windy!' she laughed as the opened door showed Angela, her hair blowing and her coat wrapping itself against her legs. It was the wind that screamed.

'I'll tell you what,' said Angela, pushing in, her hair settling back, and a glow on her cheeks.

'What?'

'I'm sick of our bloody weather!'

They both laughed, without sufficient reason, as they went on through, past the throaty clock which was about to chime half past eight. The hands might move more quickly now that there was another person in the house: they had dragged themselves around between four o'clock and eight as though more intent upon measuring irritation, and doubt, and then serious anxiety, than the minutes and quarters.

Helen had been expecting to hear from John. She did not know whether he had not called her because the meeting with the publisher had gone badly, or because it had gone well. It was not possible to telephone him, because she did not know where he was.

They (that is, he) had sold their tiny mews house in Paddington in a cobbled alley the estate agents had called Hyde Park after consulting a district map which bulged or narrowed in unrecognizable projections. And John had been so taciturn or, rather, plain morose on the morning he had left that he had not told her which hotel he was going to use. She knew that he did not have any old girlfriend to look up, and she had come to the brink of hoping that he would pick up some younger tart or other. Anything which might subvert his introspective melancholy, or soften the odd violet glare in the set of his eyes.

She also knew, though, that the solution or the alleviation did not lie between the sheets. The cause of the trouble was more likely to have begun there.

Helen, reviewing the past, his and hers, had telephoned Angela a few minutes before eight o'clock because she could no longer bear to be on her own. Waiting for the news that he had, or had not, returned to the commerce of the outside world was bad enough. She wondered whether he had sold the idea or been fobbed off, English-style, with a smile and a limp handshake.

Worse by far than the waiting was the insidious, unlocatable nervousness which had begun to gnaw at the edge of every thought and every movement. It had sneaked and whispered its way into each room of the house, into the shapes of the chairs, the pitch of the stairs, the faint hum of the refrigerator, the drip-drip of the water tank, the click of the cupboard door, everywhere. And it had fleetingly taken a human shape, corner of the eye, turn of a head, in the garden, and against the window-panes.

Nervousness was not unknown to her, even of this kind: when she was on the verge of adolescence, for instance, her mother had stayed out on a dark winter's night much later than she said she would, her father God knows where, and had come back with a whippet-faced drunk at two o'clock in the morning to find Helen lying flat out on the carpet in the cubby of a space between the sofa and the wall, paralysed with fear. It was elevated into a joke between her mother and herself, when jokes were still possible.

But this was worse, if only because she was now a mature woman. Helen did not believe herself to be especially neurotic, given the bizarre nature of the three or four years before her marriage. The worst fault she would concede in that line was the self-admission that she was an incorrigible liar.

'All right. What's the matter, darling?' Angela asked, rather unpleasantly breezy, as soon as she sat down.

Helen smiled in a fixed way at her, still standing. She went to answer, and then said something else instead: 'You don't mind something from the freezer and into the micro do you? A sort of double cheat. But we can liven it up with a bottle of wine.'

'I don't mind at all. In fact, just the wine will do.'

'Well, if you're sure. At least, it's a fairly decent wine – '

'What on earth is the matter, Helen?'

Angela was looking at Helen's hands, which were clasping and unclasping, so tightly as to make her arms stiff and her shoulders rigid. She separated her hands and looked at them, almost as though they belonged to another person, fingers extending.

'Oh, Angela,' she said, like a little girl about to burst into tears, but also as though she were preparing to laugh.

'Come on,' said Angela. 'Let's open the wine.'

'With some cheese,' Helen said, nodding and nodding, and then nodding again, at least twice too many times. 'We'll have it with some smelly old Stilton, shall we?'

Angela knew now that she was going to enjoy the evening

after all. She was not one to enjoy swapping the dirt with the girls, as the song almost had it, but the prospect of indiscreet revelation and high emotion fitted the house and the windy night. There did not seem to be any danger of herself getting hurt. John had not been one of her lovers, although she thought the possibility had flared briefly in an ambiguous conversation they once had in the doorway of the village post office, of all unlikely places. But –

'What on earth's that?' she said, suddenly startled.

'Oh. It's the useless old apple tree. It goes tap-tap like that against the window on windy nights. Just as though it wants to get in.'

'Wuthering bloody Heights,' said Angela, with such cool disdain that Helen laughed, and felt an obscure relief. She decided that she did like Angela after all.

Tell all? Tell some of it? Tell nothing?

A glass of red Burgundy, dusty brown in the throat, and then another, growing fruitier and heavier in the mouth, and on the third, which had a distinct amber glow in the head, she was letting explanations and anxieties come out across the rim of the glass. This was why she had called Angela.

As she described it, beginning with what was rational, the crucial event, the key to everything else aslant and askew, had been when John lost his terrifically well-paid job with the advertising agency he had himself founded with two of his Oxford friends before allowing it to be taken over.

But even as she said this, she realized it was not the reason. And the wayward wish slunk back into her mind that she needed a long, sharp knife on the table beside her. A weapon to pick up in an emergency. She wanted to test the edge of the blade against her thumb.

'Yes. That's not nice, the way it was done,' agreed Angela, about the dismissal, but hoping that it was not going to be a conversation about money.

Why am I thinking about a knife? thought Helen.

'It came out of the blue, you see,' she said, at the same time as the blade flashed in her thoughts. 'There was no warning. Nothing. He simply had no idea what was going on.'

'Mmm. Horrible. I can see that.'

Angela was there to prompt, not to analyse, until and if something juicier came out. She made sure that Helen's glass was kept topped up.

'There's another bottle,' said Helen.

'Good! I feel like getting a bit squiffy!'

'But – ,' the hesitation poised on the lip of the wineglass. Helen drank. Her eyes shifted. 'But it's not just that.'

'No,' said Angela, and not as a question.

They both heard the branch of the apple tree tap and then plaintively scratch at the window, and they looked at each other, and then they both laughed.

'I'd chop that bloody thing off,' said Angela, and stopped at the green and steady look which settled on her.

'Sex,' said Helen.

Well, as if I didn't know, thought Angela, with a little bump of salacious pleasure. As if it isn't always. Good old, yukky old, o-oh old sex, hello, and here we are again.

'Oh, dear,' she said, with a properly composed face.

Tap-tap and scratch went the apple tree on the pane. It did not look as though Helen, having released the little hob-goblin of a word, was going to add to it.

'Do you mean,' Angela had to ask, 'that there's someone else?'

And then Angela laughed out loud, with a whoop, though she quickly clapped her hand to her mouth, as Helen frowned and twitched a foot.

'No, no,' Angela said, embarrassed. 'It's not that – I mean, no I'm not saying that it's funny or – it's just that the question – '

'What question?' and a cold look.

'It's the one they always ask in the serials. The soaps. You know – "Do you mean there's someone else?" – ' she started to laugh again. 'It's the way it comes out.'

'Well. There isn't,' said Helen, still frowning.

Angela could see that her laugh was a great irritant, and stifled it. 'No. Of course not,' she said, in a solemn tone. 'I didn't really think there could be.'

'In some respects, it might even be better if there were.'

Ah? thought Angela, who was still finding it hard not to snigger. An inappropriate hilarity was pressing at the back of her nose like a sneeze. She drank some wine, quickly.

'But I honestly don't think he's capable of it,' Helen was saying, with a certain contradictory pride.

'No. Not John,' said Angela, at once, recalling the way he had touched her elbow in the post-office doorway, making the slim bracelets chink on her arm.

'He was always a bit of a puritan, you know. His father was a clergyman, and one of those slap-the-pulpit ones. Jesus Christ.' Helen's foot was twitching again, and her eyes looked suddenly very fierce.

'You mean he – ?' prompted Angela, who immediately wanted to laugh again. She could hear the 'You mean?' coming out in the sort of wide-eyed way she had seen in scores of television programmes. But Helen was looking too fiercely at her, and Angela realized that there was now a danger that any confidences might dry up before they had properly begun.

'When you say he's a puritan,' she said, cautiously, 'do you mean that – well, he sort of – doesn't like it? Is that what you mean?'

Helen kept the same gaze, but Angela realized that it was not particularly fixed on her. It was singling nothing out. And she was not going to answer.

'Lots of men don't, you know,' she said, again. 'I mean,

they like the *idea* of it, the little piggies – but their eyes are too big for their little whatsits.'

'What?' as though she had not been listening.

I wish I had a knife. I wish I had a knife within my reach.

'Lots of men,' Angela repeated. 'They like the idea of sex more than they actually like doing it.'

You slut, thought Helen, unreasonable. You slag. Are you trying to tell *me* about what men want and don't want? Well, listen to this, you tight-arsed little bitch, and . . .

But the violence and the crudity of her thoughts, as well as the dangerous hint that she might let out more than she intended, quickly appalled her. She could almost feel the acid breaking into tiny bubbles at the back of her tongue.

'I don't think it's like that exactly, it's not as simple as that,' she said, simulating the manner of a woman about to open her heart. 'He can be very hungry that way, in bed. Oh, that's not the right word, hungry. That's not the way to – I can't talk of these things very easily.'

My, you're a deep one, thought Angela, not sufficiently taken in. 'But no one can, Helen,' she said.

'No?' said Helen, tartly. 'Well you could have fooled me. I'm beginning to think that it's about the one and only thing people *can* talk about nowadays.'

Angela sat forward briskly at this, proffering the bottle again. Helen put her hand over the top of her glass, and shook her head, still in the same spirit as her remark, but perhaps not aware that bodily movements lie less efficiently than the tongue.

'It's when it's over,' Helen said. 'It's afterwards. Just after.'

She was not far from the truth, except that she had ignored all that was prior to the reactions she was about to describe. Her account was to be based upon one particular exchange in the early days of her relationship with John.

He had once, and with embarrassment, tried to answer her probings about an obvious sadness that had followed the vigours of their love-making. His head was on the pillow, his eyes looking up at the hotel-room ceiling, and his legs unnaturally stiff against the sheet.

There is a name for it, he had said, searching for someone to share an evident distress. There really is a name for this moment, or this condition, as it falls upon a man. He was not thinking of the expense of spirit in a waste of shame, or the other way around. He meant something both more dignified and more clinical. This feeling, he had said, speaking slowly and with reluctance, this feeling has very old labels attached to it, and noble verses, and a – well, yes, a sweet sort of melancholy.

She had no idea that men might think like this.

'But it's not natural,' she had protested, even though she had been more pleased by the discovery than not. She was willing him to look at her, already afraid that he might go away for good, and that the amazing thing she was just beginning to accept as a possibility might not happen after all.

'That is exactly the point, my love,' he had said. She was made wary by the sarcasm in his voice. She had not heard that in him before now. She moved her toe against his leg, just in case.

'What do you mean?' she had asked, but not in a plaintive way. 'How can it be the point? John. A fuck is a fuck, and – '

She stopped speaking when she saw his face. Clearly, this was the wrong thing to say.

'Sorry,' she said, and gave a sudden lick at his ear.

Instinctively he had turned his head away, and she sensed the momentary but controlled revulsion. She lay still, not hurt, but puzzled, and determined to be extra cautious.

In a little while, he had turned back to her. The tips of his fingers began to make small circles on her arm. His face lost its tightness, and his eyes seemed to go lighter in colour.

'A fuck is a fuck is a fuck,' she had said to herself, but wondering why the thought now upset her, too.

'Your arm,' he said, as though he were bananas.

'What about it?'

His fingers had stopped moving in little circles or doodles on her flesh. She knew then he was about to talk, and for some reason this alarmed her.

'Darling,' he said, and she recognized the appeal in his voice. He wanted her to understand – what?

'It doesn't matter,' she said, softly. The act of love would do. Don't talk it out of the window . . .

But he had taken a lot of words, and a lot of eye-shifting, and then a lot of moving about in the hotel room overlooking the park. She had stayed where she was, a lavender-coloured and lace-edged pillow plumped up at the back of her neck, an encouraging or interested look carefully in place, and her eyes never leaving him.

He had pulled on his underpants and then his socks with an odd little blush of self-consciousness. She watched him walk to the window and back to the end of the bed and across to the window again. She could see the tops of the trees in the park, rolling like the sea.

When, later, she had tried to remember what he had said as he moved restlessly up and down the room, it was more the tone and the wistfulness which she got hold of. She wished, now, that she had listened as carefully as she had pretended, suspecting that at least some of the clues to his recent behaviour were to be found in the words he used on that afternoon.

In essence, as she pieced it together, and missing too much, what he had said, with many hesitations and diversions, was this: some men, who knows how many, perhaps most at some time in their lives, especially when their stronger emotions are involved, feel a division in themselves which causes anguish and an impossible longing.

The division, he had said – so far as she could remember – was between the brute language of their bodies, or their physical needs, and the distant, muffled cries of 'what I have to call their spirit' or – and she *did* remember the scorn in his small laugh – or 'the soul'.

Human beings were strangers here, but did not experience this sense of loss and state of exile until something made them recognize it.

Yes. Yes. She had heard that sort of crap before, and wondered, not without reason, how it was possible to talk like this in your socks and underpants while walking up and down in a hired bedroom.

'Soul?' she had asked, the one time during any of this that she had spoken. He stopped the pacing and looked steadily at her, and she wished she had said nothing.

'Old words,' he said, 'are useful sometimes – '

Yes, she thought. Like 'fuck'. That's an old word. Anglo-Saxon.

' – because their imprecision pre-dates the scientific age which tries to narrow down and define every concept and every abstraction as if they were material things, as solid as this dressing table.'

Or something like that, as his hand came down with a smack on the laminated surface, making the mirror tremble.

'But I don't know where they came from, these feelings, and I wish I didn't have them. This sense of – this disgust . . .'

Disgust? Oh. Thank you. Thank you very much.

He said, so far as she remembered, that he did not know whether women experienced the same degree of alienation from their bodies or their physical feelings, and that he would not be impertinent enough to guess. She thought, though, that he went on to suggest that men had a less fundamental relationship than women with the natural world and its rhythms. They don't have periods, men don't, hoo, and they cannot give birth to their own kind.

'I know that,' she had wanted to say, but wisely, did not.

It was a little while after this that he had stopped the irritating pacing from window to bed to window and sat on the edge of the bed and taken hold of her hand. What had then passed between them lifted her up out of a mire she had never acknowledged as a mire. It was the hour of her personal salvation.

But she tucked this away out of her head for the moment, sitting opposite Angela, whose eyes were gleaming too eagerly.

'It's when it's over,' Helen had said. 'It's afterwards. Just after.'

She knew she was betraying him. But things had gone too far. They had to be talked about, if only in a partial or oblique and dishonest way. She needed help, and advice.

'He tried to explain it to me once,' Helen said. 'He doesn't *want* to feel what he feels. He said it was a . . . was a, sort of blackness or . . . or a despair about being separated from himself – oh, I can't put it the way he did, because it didn't make much sense to me then and it makes almost none at all now.'

'Blackness?' Angela arched her plucked brow.

'Despair,' said Helen, her mouth tightening.

'What? About a fuck?' asked Angela, looking and sounding so completely incredulous that they both laughed and agreed to have another glass of wine.

'There's some cheese,' said Helen, who had forgotten to bring it in with each of the two bottles.

'Never mind the cheese. This'll do very nicely, ta.'

Angela lifted her newly filled glass, smiling sweetly, and clearly anxious that Helen should not be interrupted.

'When we, you know, finish,' said Helen, in a rush of candour, 'he twists his head away to the side and sort of – sort of – oh, I don't know. I feel awful saying it. It's not exactly a groan or a cry. But I can see. I can tell. He's as down as down can be. Doesn't exactly make me feel great.'

'But is this always? I mean, does it happen every time?'

Helen nodded, and they were both surprised by the bright glint of tears in her eyes.

'Oh, don't,' said Angela, quickly.

'Every time is a bit of history now,' Helen said. 'We don't very much now, anyway. I mean – ,' and she stopped.

The apple tree scratched and rapped once more, and the wind which had caused it to do this moaned with another part of itself in the chimney.

Why is she looking at me like that? thought Angela, with a flurry of alarm.

'How do *you* manage, Angela? Sex, I mean. That stuff.'

Angela kept very still, listening to the wind. 'Oh, I get by, somehow or other,' she said.

Martin Stoner, for one, thought Helen. Amongst a good many others. She should charge them for it. Money for old rope.

'No, I – no, not who do you have, or anything like that,' she said, again dousing down the venom in her thoughts, puzzled by it. 'I mean, is it important to you? Can you get along without it for a long time, or – ?'

'No,' said Angela, 'I can't.'

Helen picked up her glass and put it down again.

She doesn't know she's doing that, thought Angela, the tiny spasm of something too close to fear still at work in her. She doesn't know that she's picked up and put down the glass for the third time in a few moments. And I'm not going to let on about Martin, or anybody else. I think she knows. I think she resents it. She's jealous. Christ, these wives. These bored women.

'I don't think I can very easily either,' Helen said. 'But I've had to.'

They were silent for a while. The wind seemed to have dropped, and there were no scratchings at the window or moanings in the chimney. Then Angela saw that the glint in

Helen's eyes was being overwhelmed by bigger drops, and the tears welled, trickled, and she was surprised to find that she minded Helen crying much more than she imagined she would.

'Oh, don't, darling,' she said, moving her arm so quickly that her bracelets tinkled against each other.

Sympathy can be a gross provocation in times of stress. Helen's slow tears burst into a full sob. 'Oh, Christ,' she managed, between heaves and gasps. 'Oh, God.'

'Let it out,' said Angela, unnecessarily. 'Let it come.'

But the swift upsurge of her sympathy was as fast falling back. I must always remember, she was thinking, how ugly a woman who blubs makes herself.

'It can't be as bad as you think. Honestly. It never is,' she said, and drank some wine to show it must be so.

17

The sky was darker now between the lattice of the branches, and it emptied all the sadness it had stored on to his shoulders. His feet were no longer determined to take him to wherever he was supposed to have been. The urgent tick-a-tick-a-tick had finally wound down to a stop.

He forced himself to move. An arm as heavy as stone, slowly lifting. Neck turning as though against a restraining brace. Eyes gradually fixing, but at first the hands of his watch had no relationship with each other. He studied them, rocking slowly to and fro on his heels.

Ten minutes to seven. It was hard to work this out. Some hours seemed to have gone astray, and so had too much of the light. He could not remember where he had been. Apparently, nowhere at all, since he was still in the park, and in the same place within it. But his trousers were wet at the knees, and the cloth was clinging to him. Had he flown again, beyond the darkened sky and the dripping trees? The haven to get to would be the amiable room he had seen through a window somewhere, sometime.

Fly! he said to his limbs. But they did not obey. He had forgotten how to do it, and yet he so badly wanted to find a safer and drier and friendlier place to be. What did he need to do? Fly! he urged. Soar away!

Half a pound of tuppenny rice, half a pound of – ? No. It didn't work. The silly old tune at the back of his mind only increased the suffocating sense of sadness.

I am on my own, and I am ill, he thought, but even these perceptions were oddly muffled. His brain was trying to work with dirty wadding pressed and packed around it. He could feel the stuff, thick against the back of his eyes, and going on deeper and tighter into his head.

If I could only clear it away, he reasoned. If I could get my fingernails back behind my eyes, and scratch there, and claw away the soiled padding that is packed there . . .

He did his best. It was the pain which eventually stopped him as he dug his fingers into his eyes. The trees, the ground, the sky burst into cascades and bars of light, smears and blobs of blue and orange. He cried out, and wet splattered on his cheeks, all the colours going scarlet and burning hot.

He put his hands back to his face, but to cup it, and sank down on the wet grass, writhing and sucking in his breath, hurting so badly.

In time, he lay still. It was much darker now. The shapes of the branches way above him made less certain patterns against the murky, rain-sodden light. He began to see them for what they were, uninterested in his plight, and to understand that the hum in the distance was still that of the traffic on the Bayswater Road. The branches could not talk, and the traffic did not know. He digested the thought, under the pain.

'I wonder,' he said to himself, or perhaps it was out loud, 'whether anyone will come and help me. I wonder if anyone knows where I am or what has happened to me?'

But while he was thinking or saying this, the realization sprouted little white hairs, a mere three inches from his nose. The hairs were decking a slender stem, and spreading on to wrinkled leaves *Marrubium* made letters in front of his streaming and bloodied eyes. He was holding a pencil, or so he thought, and the sharp point was going up and down, up and down, on the final letter.

'White horehound,' he breathed into the air, to test it. 'White horehound,' he said, out loud, feeling the relief invade him. '*Marrubium vulgare*. White horehound. White horehound.'

He pulled himself forward towards the wild flower. The trickle of warmth which had started in him widened and widened until it came at the full flood of an unexpected joy. Even the pain in his eyes became nothing more than a far-off distraction. The weed had vanquished it. 'Bitter juice,' he said.

White horehound, as his father had once explained, in a sermon or on one of their terrifying walks, had obtained its proper name from a Latin corruption of the Hebrew. Bitter juice. His father glimmered into his mind, like a ghost, patrolling the edge of a sloping field, insisting in a great booming monologue that it was one of the bitter herbs the Jews used to eat during Passover.

What was it doing here? How far had it wandered, and for how many years, across what deserts, what scrub, what emptiness of spirit? The bloom had small lobes, and the leaves had teeth, but it was a poor, grubby straggle of a thing, scarcely able to stand. And yet out of nowhere, with a true grace, it had given him its name.

He stretched out his hand in order to touch the leaves, not noticing the specks of blood and the smear of some sort of slime on his fingers. The most important act he could think of doing now was to rub one of the leaves into his skin, and to feel the furry white hairs, the mottle of green, and receive the faint minty odour as a balm.

But he could not seem to get a hold on it. The flower shifted out of grasp, and yet it stayed within his range.

'White horehound,' he said to it, out loud, in the hope that it would respond to its name.

'Get up! Stand up! Stand, you fool!'

The brutality of the voice surprised him. His friend did not normally address him with such little respect. Did he not know of the grief that was pressing down upon him, or of the pain in his eyes? They were burning in his head once more, smouldering holes in the bone of his face.

'Get up! Before it is too late! Get up on your feet!'

But it was no use. Neither the wild flower nor his old, secret friend could intercede. The stray weed in the park pulled itself further and further into the darkness, at the same time as the voice of the other John faded into a desperate whisper and then fell silent.

'Now, now, then,' said a wary young policeman, coming across the sodden grass in a squelch of self-parody. 'What's all this, eh? What do you think you're doing?'

John was in no condition to answer. He was conscious mostly of the burning pain in his eyes, and of endless, grey caverns of grief around and beyond whatever else he could glimmer. Wild flower, tall tree, wet grass, dark sky, and now two blue legs.

'Get up, sunshine,' said the constable, in his more usual tones, half prepared to use his boot.

John was not so far gone as not to know that this was indeed what he should do. He somehow knew, too, that the legs in front of him, uprights in cartwheels and random flashes of horizontal light, were the legs of the law of the land. There was a gap, however, between these fleeting insights and what to do with them. He tried to make his tongue work and his lips unflatten themselves from against his teeth. Out of the extremity of his need, an approximate form of speech forced itself out. 'Well aware,' he sort of said, but the policeman reacted to the noise with distaste.

'Come on. Come on, you!' he said. 'Up you get. Up you bloody well get, you hear!' and yanked him half-way off the ground in an expertly rough grip. He noticed as he did so that the bothersome nutter had good clothes, and, even now, with red and streaming eyes, enough of the bearing of a man of substance. A modicum of caution might not be out of place.

'Well aware,' said John, a little more distinctly, this time separating out the syllables into three distinct spasms which his mother might have understood.

'What's that? What you say, Jimmy?'

John steadied himself, letting his knees take the weight, and tried to point down at what he felt was significant without knowing why it was, or what he or anyone else was supposed to do about it. In any case, his hand would not obey his arm, and the fingers made a piano-playing motion.

'Horehound,' he croaked, urgently and coherently.

Oh, yes, thought the policeman. I see. Swear your head off, old son, it's that sort of fucking night. He led him, without difficulty, across the wet grass and around a puddle towards the police car waiting on the side road through the park. The dome light on the roof of the car flicked and turned and flicked, calling them in.

'Run,' said the other John, frightened.

'I can't,' said John, just as scared.

'Yes, you can,' said the constable, matter-of-fact, gripping him tightly enough on the arm to leave the shadow of a bruise for the doctor to find the next morning.

18

When Helen awoke out of a classic nightmare of screaming ghouls and glinting knives she found that she was already looking at the little clock on her bedside table. It was as though its face had been in her dream, for her eyes were fixed on it before she was aware of opening them, and it took her a moment to make her brain begin to read the hands. The clock seemed to be reluctant to let go of its simple information.

A couple of minutes, it was, before half past ten in the morning. She worked it out with a little kick of pain in the circle of bone around her thoughts. Too late to be decent. It's the drink, she thought. The bloody wine.

She was irritated by the difficulty she seemed to be experiencing in trying to take her eyes off the little clock. It had a sleek black face with white dots in place of numerals and brilliant white hands. A designer had been at it, and even without a hangover you needed to look twice to be sure of getting the time right.

When Helen did manage to look away the pattern of the clock reimposed itself for a moment in white and black against the pale blue of the opposite wall. Her head sent out another warning throb as she moved her neck on the pillow.

'Bloody drink,' she said. And, immediately, an arrow flew and struck: 'Where is he? Why didn't he telephone?' and as the head bit deeper, 'What have I done?'

Helen lay still, letting some of the throbbing pain subside. She looked up at the white of the ceiling, where speckles and dapples of light played, as on the surface of water.

'What has happened to him? Why doesn't he telephone?'

The returning questions caused her to sit up, but gingerly. Her feet searched for her mules on the floor. 'What if he means to go for good?' she thought, and her feet stopped moving.

Birds were singing outside, an idiot clamour. I'll cut their heads off, she thought, and then let the violence ebb again. A pale September sunshine, unsure of itself, was coming and going in the room. She noticed that the rays were entering at lower and lower angles as the year journeyed on. Soon, they would reach under the bed, and show gleams of dust at the bottom and back edges of dark corners.

'Please, God,' she said, out loud.

But as when she had looked on waking at the clock without seeming able to see it at once, so now did she say the words of despair before a full awareness of the enormous, billowing folds of grief which were in place and about to drop and enfold her.

They fell. Fold upon fold, softly, covering her from head to toe, so that even if she moved the smallest muscle it brushed against melancholy. A tremor in any part of her, skin or bone or tiniest rivulet of thought, would set up wider and wider ripples of despair.

And then the telephone rang.

Her hand went straight through the enveloping folds as though they had never existed. She picked up the telephone in the same swoop.

'John – ?' she said, eagerly, as soon as the mouthpiece came up.

'Helen,' said the voice, and it wasn't his voice. 'It's Martin Stoner. Hello? Helen? I hope this isn't a bad moment, or – ?'

'Martin,' she said, sick with disappointment. 'Hello. How are you?' She was surprised by how ordinary her voice sounded, and by the speed with which it acknowledged that there were other beings, other feelings, other issues in another world.

'I'm fine. I wondered if I could have a word with the Master of the House?' he said, boringly and routinely satiric.

'What?' she was finding it hard to think.

'John, my love,' said the telephone voice, in a mechanical simper. 'I presume he's bent over his daubs or whatever they are. He doesn't want to be disturbed, right? But I think he'll want to hear this. It's about the house.'

'The house?'

'Well, I told him the other day I wouldn't have to look very far to find a buyer with cash in his hand, and clever old me, I think I've already come up with – '

'Martin,' she interrupted. 'Martin. Please. What are you talking about?'

'Acre House, of course,' he said, in a changed tone. And then, 'What do you mean, what am I talking about?' and then, 'Helen?'

Tears sprang out of her so quickly that they might have been made by a bursting capsule. But she somehow managed to keep them out of her voice, although she did not speak soon enough or with a sufficiently casual intonation: 'John's not here. He hasn't come back yet.'

'Helen. What is the matter? Have I spoken out of turn? Are you saying you don't know about . . . ?'

She put the phone down before he could finish the question, and covered her face with her hands. She remained sitting on the edge of the bed, but rocking a little, without knowing it.

So it was true. It really was true. John had talked in secret to Martin Stoner about selling the house he had said at least ten times over that he loved. The roof was going to be taken from over her head. He had already worked out his plans, and none of them had been discussed with her. It was a plot, and she was its victim.

Helen bit her lower lip, folded her hands over her bare belly, where the short night-dress had reeved up, and rocked a little faster.

As she did, an image formed in her mind. It was a familiar one to her, but she had not experienced it for a long time. The picture was of herself walking down a long, dustily white road with a small case in her hand held together by double loops of thick string. There were tall poplars on either side of the road, as aloof and distinct as is their kind. Up ahead, on the endless road, the trees merged together. It was an image she used to have in the later years at school, when there was trouble at home, and sometimes, too, in the flat she had shared with another girl in London.

The telephone rang again. She picked it up without saying John's name this time.

'Helen? Why did you hang up on me like that?'

Like many who care a lot about their dignity, Martin Stoner regularly compromised it by the ease with which he took inappropriate offence. Helen now gave him better cause for complaint. Hearing the peevishness, so small in the scale against her own anxiety, she put the phone down without saying a word.

An hour later, she had drunk most of a pot of strong coffee, which had left a bitter residue in her mouth. She wanted to start smoking again, but could not find a cigarette anywhere in the house. But by now she had picked her way through the rubble to the edge of the flatter ground where things could at least be thought about.

The long stretch of poplar trees was not now distinct as an image in her mind, but each problem still stood in melancholy sequence before her, apparently going on for ever and ever, as the trees had done along the white road.

'I'll kill him,' she thought. And then, at virtually the same moment, 'I'm dependent. I have been totally dependent on him.'

The dishonesties, evasions and half-truths of her conversation with Angela the previous night came back at her. Not once, not by the smallest hint, had she told the truth about the history of their relationship and brief marriage. But how could a woman like Angela understand such things?

'I'm dependent,' she wanted to say out loud, doubly to cancel any prior and violent thoughts. 'I'm totally and for ever dependent on him.'

Her mother, entering her life again for a short and destructive interlude a few years ago, had warned her that there was 'something funny' about John, and that 'it wasn't safe to have a man who could look right through you', but her mother – although similarly disposed – did not have the faintest idea of the kind of life Helen had been leading.

Helen let a postponed question drop into her thoughts: could she return to it, that life? Her mouth tightened.

Well, it wouldn't be for the money. *I shall be all right.* It certainly would not be for any personal satisfaction, or the pleasure, except in the small change of the balance between inflicting humiliation and receiving it.

It would be where she would hide. That was the reason she had gone to the so-called escort agency in the first place, though she had understood that only when John had made her see it.

'I'll tell you this,' he had said to her, at their third or fourth meeting, and the first time she had expressed a distaste about the exchange of money, 'if I were a woman who can see what goes on in the official and above-the-ground world, and I had your history, and I looked anything like as good as you do, then I would be doing exactly what you are doing. For a time. Honestly – I would.'

Reassurance, always the reassurance, and the 'honestly' honestly meant, but always, too, the possibility of an alternative, the subtle pressure to think about what you were doing, why you were doing it, and what else you might come to think as better to do.

Gradually, and not without resistance, including mockery

and inflicting embarrassment upon him, Helen had come to see what she had been doing to herself. She then sought the change as eagerly as he could ever have wanted, even though she considered his proposal – 'It's only a contract, and could be thought of as a commercial one like any other, if that's the way you want' – could never actually *work*.

And yet until a few months ago, until he had more or less locked himself away with his weeds and wild flowers, she had been able to put away from her most of the anxieties about the improbability of their arrangement with each other.

Her assumption that they would quickly be forced apart had been replaced by an incredulity that they were getting on so well, and that their lies or omissions about how they had come to meet and marry had been so easily accepted. Perhaps most people were getting away with something by such simple bravado. It was as though her recent past, glimpsed now only in a swift and fearfully wondering glance over her shoulder, had been converted into a story or a dream.

Helen sat still, except for a small jiggling of her foot, her elbows on the kitchen table. Think! she commanded herself. Think. *Think.* By attending to her own mind – as he had said – she might be able to get hold of the reason for why things had gone wrong, and once in possession of it, change the future. 'Minute by minute. We make our lives minute by minute.' Tick bloody tock.

A fly landed, and started to crawl along the rim and then on down into her nearly empty and no longer warm coffee-cup. She watched it.

The fly stopped exploring, and began to rub its back legs together. It looks as though it's cleaning itself, she thought, but I expect it's doing something else, something it cannot help doing.

She put her hand out, but then held it still. The fly stopped rubbing its legs. 'That's me,' she thought. 'That fly is me.' She kept her hand where it was, poised for descent. The fly resumed its ramble, coming up once more to the rim of the cup.

She brought her hand down hard. The cup was knocked sideways with a startling clatter into its saucer, throwing out its half-an-inch of cold brown liquid, across the table. The fly had gone.

'That's me,' she said to herself again, imagining escape. 'That fly is me. I shall survive.'

I shall survive. I shall look as though I am cleaning myself, but I expect I will be doing something else, something I cannot help doing. So be it.

She righted the cup, and stared at it. The fly made a few routine circles and passes around her head, and then, as though conscious of her abstraction, landed once more on the rim of the cup. Its own disproportionate eyes could see all around, at all angles, but they could not, like hers, call back pictures from the past.

Which was where she was now. A slender and beautiful young woman with a vague expression walking down a long, thickly carpeted corridor, away from the triple-banked elevators, looking at numbers on the doors.

19

Penny, she called herself, or Penelope, in a classical little reversal of sorts towards her own name. She was going to meet what the others called 'the punter', a man she probably would not have seen before. It was a strange life, which was about as far as she ever went in describing it to herself. She seldom experienced either the fear or the distaste she once supposed she might have felt when going to meet the stranger. They were usually timid or gross and nothing much very interesting in between. A few make-believe coos and murmurs and pretty poutings, some strategically placed gasps, and the mauling, grappling, usually sweaty middle-aged man was over and done with. Nothing to worry about.

At times like these, coming down the ninth-floor corridor looking for the right door, it was as though she had lost touch with herself, the real woman who was surely elsewhere thinking real thoughts and doing real things.

And yet she was alert, for all the vagueness of her manner. Her eyes saw everything. Her senses were quicker than she would allow them to be. Her awareness of the differing smells, for instance, would have enabled her to chart her passage with her eyes closed. The floor and the walls sent up hotel odours. Room-service food, flowers, starched bedlinen and various cleaning fluids, crinkly leather smells, rich humans in transit, poorer maids in more hurry in smaller orbit. Her skin responded to the touch of her dress against her stockings, and to the barely perceptible currents of the air-conditioning.

She was living in the present tense. Her mind did not rake

back over what had happened, turning it this way and that. She did not anticipate, and let her thoughts curl around what might be to come. If anyone had stepped out of one of these doorways and asked her, without warning, where she lived or what she planned to do tomorrow, or even later that same evening, she would have had more than a moment's difficulty in answering.

Penny did not consider herself to be unhappy, because she did not consider what she was at all. There was no need to think in this manner. Yesterday was dead and gone, one more measure, and tomorrow was only a smudge of land on the horizon, inhabited by she did not care what. What you did in between, in these bobbing moments, had only accidental relations with either of them.

Room 923. That was what she was looking for. She had misread the indicators opposite the lifts, and walked three-quarters of a circle, instead of a quarter of one.

Penny, as she was then, four years ago, in high summer and her later twenties, tapped discreetly on the door and then stood back a foot or so, a smile in place, and her chin tilted a little. Misleadingly looking like a girl about to hum a catchy tune.

While she waited, she tried to measure the depth of the deceptive glint on the bronzed numbers. She also watched the fluted coils go round and round the fat and purely decorative doorknob. And then she let her eyes steady, and settle on the circle made by the spy-hole in the middle of the silvery grey wood of the door. There would be, she knew, another eye placed close to it on the other side, checking on her, examining the goods.

Hurry up, she thought. Hurry along, if you please.

Her smile wavered. She shifted on her high heels, went to look at her wrist-watch, stopped herself, and tapped again with the crook of her long fingers, a little more loudly, but not enough to give cause for fuss.

This kind of nuisance happened from time to time. There could be a mix-up in the details given to her over the telephone, rarely to the wrong hotel, but to the wrong room. The punter could get too nervous, or have an unexpected visitor.

But she had always been warned not to draw too much attention to herself by banging or ringing on the door too insistently, and certainly not by trying to call through it. It was not even the right thing to telephone up from the lobby.

Penny waited for another six, seven, eight beats, counting them, adding one more, then smiled sweetly at the peep-hole just in case it made any difference, and turned away.

Oh, well, doesn't matter a damn, she thought, going the shorter way back to the elevators. A room-service cart, in which sticks of celery protruded, was being pushed towards her by a surprisingly old and worn-out floor waiter for a hotel as expensive as this one. His pinched and tobacco-ash face, and shifty, vaguely yellow eyes needed his working smile of subservience to make him look even half-way respectable. The smile was not at the moment in operation.

Penny met his furtive glance, and ignored it. He knows, she thought. The little weasel.

'I'm sorry,' said a mild voice behind her. The floor waiter swivelled his eyes off her, and put on his smile, going on past her.

Helen, who was not given to reverie, had several times tried to bring back the detail of this moment. She was doing so now, her elbows on the kitchen table, an emptied cup before her, and a fly making circles above her head. There was a crunch of feet on the gravel outside, but she did not hear it.

The one sound she was picking up, apart from the 'I'm sorry' was the slight and almost musical creak of the room-service trolley as it went on its way down the long corridor. There was a bird in the garden which sometimes made the same sort of noise, and now caused her to tilt her head in the middle of other activities.

She was remembering now, how she did not think that the voice could be addressing her: the tone was not right, somehow. She had been used to a different style of approach, the one with the half-proprietorial, half-hopeful, in-built leer. The way men talk to women when they imagine the conventions no longer apply, conventions they have themselves built in order to mask by politeness and economics the nature of their dominance and their determination to keep things just exactly so.

'I'm sorry.' Two words can be enough to signal an authentic gentleness, even in middle-class English English where the norm itself is modulated into a very good imitation of the same elusive grace.

'I suppose you must have known very well that someone was looking at you through one of those peep-hole things in the door,' he said, the man coming up alongside her in the hotel corridor, the man who became John.

'Sorry?' she said, being cautious. She assessed him quickly. A tall, lean-faced and rather bony man a bit older than she was, with the slight stoop which diffident men often have to bring themselves back down to the six-foot mark. She presumed that he had caught sight of her through the little fish-eye viewing hole in one of the doors opposite. It did not cross her mind, though it was by far the most likely explanation, that he was the punter, the stranger, the waiting client of Room 923.

'I looked at you standing there, and I'm afraid I lost my nerve. You looked so much more vulnerable than I had expected. As though you had a secret little tune in your head. I – well, I decided not to open my door. That was very rude. I'm sorry.'

She was astonished, but not so much so that she stopped walking. They had arrived at the elevators. There were other people in sight now, and probably in earshot. Half amused, and a little annoyed, she gave him a glittering, sidelong glance. One of her specialities.

'Have you changed your mind? Do you want me to come back to your room?' she asked him, in a quiet voice.

'No,' he said, firmly, and pressed his thumb on the call button. It jumped into light. His eyes shone, as though with laughter.

'That's all very well – ' she started to say, but without real indignation.

'I don't want to let you down, of course,' he interrupted, with the amusement still in his expression. 'I wondered if we could have a drink in the bar downstairs, or perhaps – '

'Money,' she said, without any answering amusement.

She heard the growing swishing noise of one of the lifts rising to meet them. It seemed to measure and to mimic the change in his expression.

'I beg your pardon,' he said.

The arriving lift went ting!, and she said, 'Money, honey,' in a deliberate parody, and rubbed the tips of her fingers together.

His face darkened, but so fleetingly that it might have been no more than the slight change of light as the small call button in the wall flicked off. The lift doors hissed open, a couple got out, and his expression was exactly the same as it had been before.

'Oh, yes. Naturally. That goes without saying,' he said, taking hold of her arm in the way a proper escort would, and guiding her into the lift. 'I don't see why my indecision should leave you out of pocket.'

Once inside he carefully separated himself from her and stood with his back against the wall of the descending box. His eyes stayed on her. She felt slightly uncomfortable under such a steady scrutiny, especially as he seemed to be quietly amused.

'It's a nice evening,' she said, lamely. He laughed.

Fortunately, more people got on at a lower floor, and began examining them in a furtive, peculiarly English style, half ready to half smile or to dart their glances away to their shoes or to the ceiling. It was a little after six o'clock in the evening, and the big hotel was becoming more active. Another few people came into the lift on the second floor, and looked at her.

He took no notice of anyone else, not once taking his eyes off her during the interrupted descent. They were so vividly blue, those eyes, that she thought of them as violet: and the word, by rubbing against another of similar sound, gave her a pang of anxiety. She smiled back at him across the crowded lift, and explained the small swoop in the pit of her stomach by the too rapid descent between the second and ground floors.

The lobby was a mill of people. Most of the voices sounded American, except for an occasional native bray.

'If it don't list what's in it, how do you know it won't trigger your allergy?' a man was saying to his wife, with signs of an irritation which must have had another cause.

The punter's hand was on her arm again. She was being steered to the left, through the sudden press of people. 'I know where the bar is,' she said, feeling suddenly unfriendly, and he immediately took his hand away. She wished that she had not spoken, and the wish puzzled her, making her look sidelong at him again as they went up a couple of wide and softly clad steps to the cocktail bar.

'As in an old film,' he said to her as they entered.

'Sorry?'

And then she understood what he meant, for as though to herald their arrival and elevate them beyond the status of mere extras, the nightly piano player began his work before they could find an unoccupied table and a couple of reasonably private seats.

A head without much hair shone over the top of the piano. Out of sight, his fingers were at least four too many as he rippled with an excess glissando or so through what she later recalled as the hat-and-coat song: the name she had always given to 'On The Sunny Side Of The Street'.

> *Take good care of yourself*
> *You belong to me . . .*

The seats sighed when sat upon. The table was awkwardly just below knee height. It had a thick, smoky glass top which sent back glimmerings of the drinks upon it, and ghostlier echoes of the elaborate ceiling, where plaster cupids sported in plaster rose arbours. The sooner the pianist got to 'Fly Me To The Moon' the better everyone would feel, without knowing why.

'A Campari,' she said, 'with a small Perrier, and lots of ice.'

He had not taken his eyes off her. The waiter had to ask him a second time what he wanted. She wouldn't have minded putting the question to him herself.

Penny looked around as she waited for him to begin the conversation. Several men in the bar, some of them with companions, crossed glances with her, but she was used to that. Beyond them, a long and slowly curving window faced out on to the park, which looked dark green in the summer evening. She turned, and saw that he was looking at the park, too, but with an expression which seemed to suggest that he was sorry for the bit of country trapped within the city. She wondered when he would begin.

'Are you here on a business trip?' she asked eventually, in the orthodox fashion, since he still showed no signs of talking.

'Don't,' he said, very quietly.

His face was blade-like now, and his knees poked up too stiffly in the low, leathery chair. The humour had gone. She could see that he was extremely tense. There's something out of line here, she thought. She put her hand on his arm and leaned into him so that no one else would be able to hear. A few things needed to be spelt out.

'You have to give me forty pounds for the agency, if they didn't tell you that – '

He pulled away a little, but kept his eyes on her, shaking his head. She smiled her sweetest and most innocent smile, and nodded. 'Whatever else you may care to give me is a personal transaction between you and me.'

Like a roll of ten-pound notes stuck together with saliva. Like the clap. Like a diamond ring, or a weekend in Paris, or a black eye, or the fraudulent offer of a share in a racehorse. Like tears of anguished self-accusation from a fruit importer who was at the same time trying his damnedest to urinate over her in a bathroom at one of the most staid hotels in London.

'There's no hurry, is there?' he asked, politely. 'I mean, I don't see this ending right here and now, tonight, or tomorrow, or anything like that.'

He picked up his drink, and smiled into it.

20

Even now, bereft in what might not be for much longer her own kitchen, Helen had to hold back a little yelp of laughter as she remembered the mild way in which he had said, 'There's no hurry, is there?' and the incredulity she must have shown as he continued.

'Whatever else you may care to give me is a personal transaction between you and me.' The swallowed laughter turned into the smaller twitch of the lips of irony's allowance. The sad-faced fellow without eyebrows who ran the escort agency had insisted that each one of the girls said that, each time, word for word, in front of any other business. The sentence, once clearly enunciated and unambiguously accepted, stood between him and a prosecution for living off immoral earnings.

'Girls, girls,' he used to say, spreading his hands. 'I ask you. Are you common prostitutes? Am I a pimp?'

But the sentence, delivered by rote, had not warded off the enemy. The police had got him in the end. She had read a long account of his trial in the newspapers in the week before John had driven back from London and told her, in tones she could hardly recognize, that he was out of a job.

'The girls,' as she still thought of them, had called the agency proprietor the Maltese Falcon. Why, she could not imagine. He was not Maltese, so far as she knew, and his eyes were watery and myopic. But the papers, too, had taken up the name with glee, for it added to the pungency of the case. Hints and innuendoes prickled against the facts in the columns. Famous Names were alleged to have been 'the clients' in a list kept by the Falcon but, disappointingly, not disclosed in the court. TWO IN A BED AND THE JUDGE said a tabloid headline, promising more than it delivered, as may have been the case originally.

Helen had let her thoughts take her away from the part of all this which lay most heavily upon her. Never mind the pathetic Maltese Falcon and his sensational trial, that was now of no importance. She had to get herself ready for a new life again.

'Or the old one,' she said.

Once said, she could no longer bear to sit still, elbows on the table. She did not know exactly what she was waiting for, except that whatever was coming was bound to be bad. It seemed essential that she move. Memory, so long suppressed or subverted, was now like a motor for her, driving her where she did not want to go.

Helen glimpsed the dusty white road again, lined with tall poplars, and herself walking along it with the battered suitcase, the rejected one with far to go.

Already, she was out in the garden, beyond the tealeaf-coloured tree, and approaching the pond. The sun, lower angled and softer, was making blobs and spangles on the water. The wind of the previous night had gone howling off somewhere else.

'Whatever else you may care to give me is a personal transaction between you and me.' How many times had she said it? How many times might she have to say it again?

There was a stale and rancorous smell coming across the glossed water from the thick green sludge that crept out beyond the reeds on the far side of the pond. She wondered what it would be like to let that stuff close over her head, a personal transaction, the last one.

'That smell,' she thought, suddenly stiffening. Was it after all from the sludge?

She was puzzled by how silent the birds had become, and

how still the air. Time itself seemed to have gathered into a single droplet of leftover moisture in the air. She had to get back into the house before the small, glistening globule fell.

'Plop!' went the water.

So strong was her sense that a stone had been tossed into the pond that she spun around, expecting to see someone.

'Plop!' went the water, now behind her.

There was nobody in sight. Everything was still and silent and luminous, tinged with a faint yellow, as though there were a quality in the air which was striving to become material. Helen felt it there, hovering before her, on the edge of change, the brink of speech. It was not something: it was someone.

'Plop!' went the water, for the third time.

Helen stood as still as she could. The only thing which moved on her was a net of prickles on her skin.

'Hello?' she said eventually, and tremulously.

PLOP! went the water, much louder than before. A bird swooped down, skimmed the surface, and flew away again.

The child should have been born, she thought. It should have lived.

21

'There's no hurry, is there? I mean, I don't see this ending right here and now, tonight, or tomorrow, or anything like that.'

She gaped, wondering what on earth he could mean, as he smiled down into his glass.

Oh, you smart-arse, she thought. You clever shit. Very funny. Then he looked straight at her, and his smile had gone.

'I wanted once to be a great artist,' he said, abruptly.

'Con artist, do you mean?' she asked, and not smiling either.

'I meant it. I'm afraid I mean what I am saying,' he said, not dropping his gaze. 'If not a great, then at least a considerable one. Not just accomplished, you understand.'

He clapped his glass down hard on the table. Such odd words, combined with such irrelevant decisiveness, made her laugh politely, on the assumption that the joke was intended.

'But I'm not good enough. I'm not quite up to it,' he said, as seriously as before.

'Oh,' she said. What the hell – ? 'That's a pity.'

'It was a pity while it remained a disappointment. But not now it isn't. You could almost say it was a relief. What about *you*? What is your disappointment in life – your major one, I mean? If I may ask.'

Well, now. How many fingers have you got? 'Well, now,' she said, instead, 'I don't think there's any one special thing. Perhaps – um – not being able to play a musical instrument.'

'Which?'

'Sorry – ?'

'Which one? Which instrument are you disappointed at not being able to play?'

'Oh. Any one. Violin. Piano. Mouth organ. You name it.'

He looked at her steadily. She smiled back at him, and felt a fool. It appeared that his question was a genuinely serious one.

'And not getting more than three O levels,' she added, much to her own surprise. 'I hated that. I hadn't worked, but I thought I was worth more.'

'Which?'

'Sorry – ?' Christ. This was hard work.

'Which three?'

Penny did not know whether to reply or not. An answer might be considered to come under the heading of Personal Information. You built a high stone wall around that, and then set jagged chunks of broken bottle-glass into concrete all along the top of the wall, and then let prickling blackthorn spread out along the ground on both sides of it. She had seen a house like this every day that her father had taken her hand-in-hand to the primary school. The walled house was always the one in her mind when she read or recollected the story of Sleeping Beauty and the Prince who hacked his way through to her.

So she said, 'Sorry?' again, half to see what he would do. He sighed, as she thought he would.

She held the cool bitterness of the pretty Campari in her mouth for a moment, and looked away to the long window and the dark green beyond it. The thought came with the distant view of the park: he means this, he is not just talking, there is something else going on. The piano player, tinkling through the standards, made a bridge and crossed from 'On The Sunny Side of the Street' into 'Stardust'.

'English Language,' she said, suddenly. 'English Literature.

161

And French.' And felt bereft. It was as though she had handed something across to another, without knowing its value. How odd, she thought. What is the matter with me? Is it 'Stardust', or – ?

He looked pleased. Why? 'And you didn't want to go on with it? School, I mean. A levels, college, all that?' he asked, again as though it were important.

'No. I – ' and then she stopped, and picked up her glass.

'Where did you go to school?'

She looked hard at him, then put down her glass, though not with quite the clap he had made. The ice went chink-chink.

'In England,' she said.

'I see,' and he was smiling. 'You don't want to tell me. But I'm afraid I can guess at the kind of school you went to. I can hear it in your speech.'

'Oh, can you?' Fucking cheek.

'You went to a private school of some sort. A school for girls. Or perhaps I should say, for young ladies.'

She said nothing. Fuck you, she thought. Fuck you, you nosy bastard! An old rebellion whirled up in her out of next to nothing, and absolute, unreasoning hatred against this sort of talk, behind which she could hear other voices that she imagined she had banished for good and all. Fuck you!

She leaned forward, the hatred reaching her eyes and the set of her long neck, speaking loudly enough for the three men at the next table to hear her, and knowing that her movement was in any case likely to draw their eyes, which had already covertly examined her several times over.

'We ought to settle here and now how much you're going to give me. I'm not going to talk about school or anything else until I know I'm not wasting my time,' she said, gathering up some mixed nuts from the glass dish on the table. Before he could say anything, she put a piece of Brazil nut in her mouth and, with a crunch, asked him whether he preferred oral intercourse or a good, old-fashioned, straight up and down fuck.

The neighbours stopped talking.

But the punter kept going, she had to give him that. His face coloured up, he shifted his knees, lifted his glass and started to shake his head, yet he did not stop, nor otherwise acknowledge the grossness of what she said.

'I think that is one of the fundamental troubles with England, your country and mine,' he said, solemnly addressing himself neither to oral sex nor to any more conventional form of fornication. 'A question about schooldays is in reality almost always seen as a hidden pointer to something else. For generations, we have placed the emphasis on the way one speaks and the way one behaves. We're most of us – or the privileged of us – we're brought up to give much more weight to what we *are* in life than what we *do* in life. Yes?'

He looked at her, his flush fading. She could see that, after all, there was desperation in his eyes. He was crying out to her not to go any further with the humiliation. She lurched inside herself, but stared back at him, expressionless.

'I mean – speech, clothes, manners, whether something is napkin or serviette, a lavatory or a toilet – all of that stuff.'

'I – yes. I suppose so,' she said, in a small voice, needing more time to work out what her response should be, but then glaring at the three men, who could not take their greedy eyes off her.

'That is what makes England feel as though it is two such opposing places – the one civilized, maybe the most civilized in the world – '

'More so than Australia?' she asked, to make him laugh, and thus to see that she was sorry for the spasm of hatred that had embarrassed him and which would cost her at least a hundred pounds.

'And then there's the other England,' he said, with a twitch of the lips. 'Complacent. Smug. Morbidly sentimental, and wallowing in a snobbish and suffocating nostalgia. Where it is possible, for instance, to believe it smart to make jokes about vulgar Americans or crude Australians.'

She looked at him. 'Canada,' she said, straightfaced. 'I meant the Canadians.'

He sat back, and looked up at the ornate ceiling. And then he laughed.

'Bravo!' she thought, relapsing into the language of her earlier days.

His smile was still in place when he sat forward again, and looked at her. 'I grieve for my country sometimes,' he said, and there could be no doubt that he meant it. The very ridiculousness of it touched her. She was astonished by him, and found that she could not stop staring at him. He did not seem to know the normal rules of ordinary conversation, let alone know how bizarre it was to talk to a call-girl about these things in this manner in this place.

'Listen,' she said, 'I'm sorry.' She touched his knee, briefly.

'Yes,' he nodded. 'I can see you are. Thank you.'

She felt the kick of obscure anger again, but was able to control it this time. 'You reminded me of – of somebody else, that's all. Asking that stuff about school and – oh, all that shit.'

'Do you normally speak like this? I mean, in your private life. Do you use gutter language there, too?'

She considered whether to get up and walk out, or to throw drink into his face and then walk out. Neither happened. He had spoken without contempt. He showed no anger. It was hard for her to puzzle it out.

'What sort of hypocrite are you?' she said, instead.

'A mealy-mouthed one,' he said, and he laughed in the kind of way which disarmed her. Who was this fellow? What did he want with her? Should she be alarmed by any of this?

'When I asked you where you went to school,' he said, as though responding to her shift of thought, 'I didn't want to know the name of the school or anything like that. Those sort of things you'll tell me over the course of time, when you want me to know everything about yourself – '

'Oh, will I?' she managed, more and more astounded.

' – I meant, which part of the country was it?'

She tried to gather her thoughts together. It was a long time since a man had so quickly unsettled her. Usually, she took no notice of them at all, even in what are supposed to be the most intimate of situations.

'Why?' she asked, combatively. 'Why does it matter? How can that be of any interest to you? Is it any of your business?'

'Oh, yes,' he said, with a nod, infuriatingly sure of himself.

The three men at the next table were still staring at her, their own conversation reduced to an intermittent and un-involved burble. Her skin was beginning to feel hot and sticky, and the piano music was starting to fret at her. There were too many sounds, too many distractions. She wanted to concentrate.

'It isn't that it's important in itself,' he was saying, 'but I thought it might be better for both of us if you hadn't gone to school in Gloucestershire.'

'?' said her face. Maybe this was one of those tedious rambles into a shaggy-dog story.

'I don't think I'd mind all that much if some of the people I know had also come across you as a child or a teenager. But you see they might also have found out what happened to you later – the kind of things you do now, I mean. I suppose that could cause some difficulties. For you, at least.'

While he said these incomprehensible words, his face was warming in the slowest of smiles. She frowned back at him, suspecting that he was laughing at her.

'And then there's the question of the O levels, too. We mustn't forget those. English Language. English Literature. French.'

'What?' and what? and what?

'Well, the fact that they might know you've only got those three. I tell you, there are savages around the dinner tables within a twenty-mile radius of Cheltenham. They are quite capable of talking about Christian Dior or Law and Order, and then where are you?'

He pulled his lips in, and she saw that he did this in order to stop laughing out loud. The light in his eyes made her want to smile too, even though she had no idea what he was talking about.

And then his face changed. He looked straight at the three men at the adjoining table, whose interest in the two of them, or mostly her, had not in the least diminished.

'Is there something you want?' he said, very loudly.

They were appalled by the brusqueness of the question and their own vulnerability to it. Each one of them jerked at the waist or the hip, and gobbled and goggled, and tried too halfheartedly to look away.

'Sorry?' said the quickest or the boldest of them, affecting not to understand.

'You seem to be more interested in what is going on over here than in your own affairs. Would you like to sit with us?'

They looked at each other, awkwardly, and began to talk, as though they were continuing a conversation that had held all their interest. She knew that they would leave within the minute, their drinks abandoned.

'Well, well,' she said, to stop him glaring at them.

'Money,' he said abruptly, turning to her. 'Let's talk about how much you would like, and what you will do to get it.'

And he spoke as clearly and as openly as though no one were in earshot at all. It made her want to let out a scream.

22

The past can sometimes be glimpsed as easily through a train window as in the pages of a family photograph album. John, rediscovering the pleasures of the railway, was almost glad that the loss of his job, from the company he had helped to found, had forced the sale of the car. The rhythm of the train, the passage of the fields and trees and house backs, reached into him, and soothed.

'I have been working too hard,' he decided.

But the work was good. He knew it was. Acknowledging this, he felt some of his recent dull heaviness begin to recede. The late sun, low on the other side of the carriage, made the shadow of the train speed alongside his window. An open field clattered by. He could see his own shape within the shadow, for a few seconds.

'I have been working too hard.'

Leaf, stem, bud and bloom. Stretch of stone wall, patch of grass, and muddy gleam of ditch. He had painted all these things, in the best pieces of work he had ever accomplished.

'It's good,' he said to himself, and looked, as he thought it, for the shadow racing along beside him.

'I have been working too hard.'

Leaf, stem, bud and bloom. 'The unregarded byways', his father had called them. Tansy came back to him, as his eyes swivelled in search of the shadow. It seemed to have separated itself from the train. A dark hump rolling through the meadows.

'That's not a shadow,' trickled a thought, out of a crevice in his mind.

He had not reached tansy yet in his long haul through all the native wild flowers. There had been too many interruptions, like that stupid dinner party.

So Martin and Angela were screwing each other, were they? Amazing how it is the little things which give people away.

Careful came out of the same crevice as before. *Be careful.*

He wondered which one had first signalled a sexual interest to the other, and how. He wondered where they managed to do it. He thought about Angela. A thin and brittle woman with enormous eyes and a wide mouth. Most men would consider her to have the promise of eroticism in her. He found her faintly repellent. There was a perpetual hint of moisture about her lips: it looked as though she had just eaten something a little greasy. Her eyes reminded him of a moth, or of the light which drew the moth, or of –

Tansy grew again. Its odours were used once upon a time to keep the flies off the meat.

He tensed at the sudden, unbidden image of his pencil inscribing the word odour on one of his index cards. And then he realized that the hand holding the pencil, and jabbing hard down with it, was not exactly his own hand.

'No,' he said to himself with determination. 'No!'

Images such as these had been flying up at him out of nowhere for days past, or perhaps weeks. He had known ones similar to these in his childhood, but then they were only a game, a defensive stratagem. Their return now, while he was working so well and with such a sense of purpose, had no justification. They were alarming. They had to be stopped.

The pictures in his head – for they were more than thoughts – had an almost luminous clarity, in which first this then another detail glowed, picking themselves out for particular attention, turning and preening before fading away again. If he were not careful, they could overwhelm him.

No, no, I am just tired. It is not surprising I am tired. I have been overdoing it.

And then, on top of everything, there was the question of Helen. Every day, every night, he thought about what was happening to her, and what he could or should do about it. Had she always been mad? Or had he been too slow to register the change?

He forced her away from his mind, for the thousandth time in this day alone, and stared through the train window, without looking at anything in particular.

Oh, the mad, he thought, *how cunning they are.*

The last call had just been made for seats in the dining car. He suppressed the rise of panic by considering whether he wanted food and drink.

Meat? The odours of tansy. Meat? Angela.

Angela. She had three thin bracelets on her arm when she came to dinner at Acre House. They clinked together when she was animated. Angela used many gestures when she talked. Her fingers were exceptionally long, and tapered to polished nails in a way that you had to find . . .

In a way that you had to find exciting.

The rest of her, no. Not so far as he was concerned. No.

But what if those hands, those fingers, took hold of you? He got up to go to the dining car. He felt a tearing sensation in his chest as he did so, and stopped for a moment, the breath hissing out of him.

John's secret friend, who had been feeling excluded and disowned, was deciding not to go to the dining car.

'Silly fool,' he called up the aisle as John went on his way again. 'Angela should be fucked! And not just by Martin. Why didn't *you* have a go?'

Angela would be more of a whore between or on the sheets than Helen could ever imagine how to be.

'Think about what you want! Look after yourself!' shouted

the other John, louder now, as the automatic door into the next carriage shushed open.

Angela's bracelets clinking and chinking together as her long fingers moved up and down, slow and then fast and then slow, making you slippery, and then her head coming over, her moist lips replacing her fingers, and the fall and quiver of her neat little breasts seen through the angle of her arm.

Oh, fly! Soar! Float! Ejaculate.

He came down without a bump into an enclosing softness. It was dark. There were strange sighs and snorts and groans all around, from unseen creatures, big beasts foraging in the night. They frightened him.

There was a glow in the distance, on his left, which formed itself into a strange kind of lamp. In a moment, as his eyes grew accustomed to the place, he made out that the odd shape of the lamp, and its shadows, was because a hand-kerchief had been draped over the shade. The already dim night-light was shedding even less of a glow than it should.

The sighs and the groans were the noises of people, not animals. Fear left him, to be replaced by bewilderment.

He was in a bed, one among many, in a long dark cavern, in the middle of the night. Clearly, a hospital ward. At the far end, slumped over the dim lamp, a nurse sat at a table. She was not moving.

'What a peculiar dream,' he thought, moving his legs against the bedclothes.

He soon realized that he was not marooned in a dream at all. Two beds away, on the other side of the doors, a man had started to grind his teeth in his sleep. Other sounds, other shapes emerged into sense. John braced his legs against the undersheet, to stop them trembling. He wanted to call out to the nurse at the top end of the ward, but he suppressed the cry. First, it was necessary to think.

The last thing he could remember was leaving his seat on the train in order to go to the dining car. The automatic doors had shut behind him, and he had peered the length of the rocking carriage, trying to locate an unoccupied window seat at the white-clothed tables.

He concentrated on the precise sequence. Had there been a train crash? No recollection of flying glass or screams or a tilting carriage came to him. The very last thing he was able to place was the view through the train window: a horse cropping grass in a field, a single dead elm. And then – this: the hospital bed, in darkness and mystery.

'Nurse!' he called, but not loudly enough. The word clogged in his throat as, at the same time as he called, the explanation for everything dropped into place.

The worst thing he could do would be to draw attention to himself. Careful. Careful. Oh, be careful . . .

23

'Gone. Gone. Gone,' Helen sang in a thread-the-needle monotone as she turned around and around. 'He's gone, gone, gone.'

These movements helped her to keep down the worst of the grief. Anxiety became rhythmic, and rhythm held the promise of monotony.

'Gone. Gone. Gone.' she sang, over and over, turning again and again in the central space between the soft chairs of the living-room. Turning and chanting and turning and chanting until eventually she achieved what she wanted, a form of oblivion, a variety of ease.

Thus, she did not hear the crunch of car wheels on the gravel outside, nor the heavy knocking on the front door. It was only after Martin Stoner had rapped many times, and sharply, upon the window by the flowerbed and the apple tree that she became aware of an intrusion. She stopped in mid-turn and on a 'Gone', seeing the shape at the window. At first, panic rushed through her, and her hand flew to her mouth, but when she recognized Martin she coloured in a helpless embarrassment. She knew what she must have looked like: insane. Martin's face, peering in with a frown of incredulity, confirmed that this was so.

Helen made an awkward gesture to tell him that he should go back around the side of the house to the front door again. He did not seem to understand the flail of her arm, which made her feel even more ridiculous. But then he nodded, still frowning, and went away from the window.

She had a few seconds in which to try to compose herself,

but the blush was too fierce to disappear in time. When she opened the front door, her face hot and the twist of a would-be rueful grin making her embarrassment even more obvious, Martin thought he had never seen her more beautiful.

'I'm sorry if I – I mean, I didn't mean to spy on you or anything like that,' he said, almost as flustered as she was.

Insane shouted the back of her head.

'I must have looked very silly,' she said, in almost a natural voice.

'No, no,' he lied, his smile too fixed.

'My exercises,' she said.

'Oh? I shouldn't think you'd need to do that, not with your figure. I mean, there can't be an excess ounce on you – '

'It's – a sort of yoga. A what do you call it, a mantra.'

'Oh. Yes. Of course,' he said, relieved. 'I understand they are all the fashion now. Help you think, isn't that it?'

'Meditate,' she said. 'Lose yourself. In a manner of speaking.'

But she was still holding the door, and he was still on the step, and each of them stayed embarrassed. They looked at each other.

'Um,' he said, and moved his weight from foot to foot.

'Martin. I'm sorry,' she said. 'Please come in.'

As she led the way, he had the chance to keep his eyes on the small sway of her hips, and the long flanks of her legs, and even to wonder if she could be approached sexually. Martin spent many minutes in each day either welcoming or trying to fend off such thoughts, never quite sure whether to celebrate himself as one hell of a dog or excoriate himself in more or less the same terms.

Seated opposite her now, he was enchanted by her febrile condition. Everything about her glowed with a vulnerability he had never seen before: Helen always seemed to him to be a little too composed, or too cold, and as smooth as an eggshell. He presumed that that was why she was not generally liked.

173

'I came over,' he said, with what he considered to be a winning smile, 'because I was hoping John would be back by now, and – '

'No. He isn't.'

He noticed the way she went to clasp her hands and then stopped herself.

'Helen. When I telephoned a couple of hours ago – '

'No,' she said. 'He isn't.'

Martin turned off his winning smile, surprised more by the tone than the repetition.

'Helen. There's something wrong, isn't there?'

She stared at him, making him feel gross. But even then, shifting uncomfortably, he did not seem able to take his eyes off the top button of her blouse, which was undone. The small pearly circle of the button shone in the light from the window, like a tiny brooch.

'Excuse me,' he said, when she did not speak. 'I don't want to poke my nose in, but I couldn't help wondering after I'd called you this morning whether there was something – well – Helen. You didn't seem to know that John had asked me to put this house on the market.'

'No. I didn't.'

He waited, but she said no more. Her hand went to the top of her blouse, and he wondered whether he had stared too obviously. She fiddled with the exposed button, as though trying to twist it off, but her eyes showed that her thoughts were elsewhere.

'I'm sorry,' he said, 'I wouldn't have dreamed of saying anything about it if I'd had any idea. I'm sure he's – John is bound to talk it over with you. I expect he's just using me to see how much you could get for Acre House if you ever . . .'

He trailed off as he watched her hand slip down to the second button on her blouse, and undo it.

'He's not coming back. He's gone. He's left me.' Each

174

sentence bleak and emphatic, and her fingers twisting and turning at the loosened second circle of pearl.

'I can't believe it,' he said, his eyes popping.

Helen sighed, and said nothing. Her skin had lost its blush, and her eyes their embarrassed anxiety. She looked totally composed once again, but detached, almost indifferent, her gaze steady yet not seeming to be settling on anything in particular.

What is she doing? he thought. *Does she know?*

When she began to undo the third button, Martin stood up, and then immediately sat down again.

'Helen,' he said, severely. 'What are you doing?'

A glint of almost malicious amusement crossed her face, so swiftly that he might have imagined it. She was looking straight at him now, with no hint of abstraction, and her hand was still at the third button, twisting it.

'You saw him here at dinner the other night,' she said. 'He could hardly be bothered to open his mouth, could he? Well, that's what he's been like for months. It's me. It's my fault. He despises me. And I can't say I blame him.'

'Helen,' he said, heavily, conveying maximum reproof, for what else could he do? He was uncomfortably aware of his erection.

'It was too much for him in the end.'

Martin's throat was beginning to tighten and to dry. Her fingers had moved down to the next button, and he could already see much of her breasts.

'What was?' he asked, with more of a comical sort of croak than he had intended. He cleared his throat, and said it again.

Helen stopped playing with the fourth button. She sat absolutely still. Her eyes did not move, staying on his now slightly flushed face. She seemed to be considering something very seriously.

'My past was,' she said, eventually. 'What I used to be.'

175

'I'm sorry, Helen. But I've no idea what you are talking about.'

She laughed, and sat back more in the chair, arching her back, a movement which thrust her hips forward. It was like the first part of a complicated keep-fit exercise.

'Christ,' he said. 'Don't do that, please!'

'What's the matter, Martin? Am I upsetting you, or something?'

He wasn't sure of her tone. She had laughed, and her words were coy, and the way she had moved her limbs downright provocative, but there was a gleam in her eyes which he could not interpret. It might be an invitation. It might be amusement. More probably, it was malice, though he saw no reason why there should be any.

'Well, I don't know about upsetting me,' he said, being careful, 'but it's not fair on a fellow to sit like you're sitting, Helen.'

'My past,' she said again, with the smallest uproll of her eyes.

'Sorry?'

'What I used to be,' she repeated, but this time she put the tip of her tongue to her lips, briefly, in what would have been a parody had it stayed there one moment longer.

Martin swallowed, and reviewed all the possibilities.

'John,' he said, even drier in the mouth.

'Gone. He's gone, gone, gone.'

'Yes, but – ' and another swallow. 'When do you expect him back?'

'Gone,' she said, in the same monotone. 'He's gone, gone.'

Martin moistened his lips. He could not quite get rid of the fear that, in some complicated way he had yet to fathom, he was being laughed at.

'I still don't follow,' he said, badly imitating an earnest frown. 'When you say Your Past and What You Used To Be, what on earth do you mean?'

Helen seemed to consider the matter again.

'Has John never, ever told you anything about the way he first met me? I mean, any hint of it. Any allusion?'

'No. I don't think so. I don't remember so.'

She stared at him as though he were lying. He twitched a little. 'No,' he reasserted. 'He never has, Helen.' What on earth was she getting at? He was so puzzled that he momentarily forgot his erection.

'No jokes? No little snides? No sniggers?'

'Helen!' he protested. 'John has never spoken of you in anything like that way. Certainly not to *me*, and I'm sure to nobody else. I don't know what the trouble is between you two, if there is any, but – '

'I don't see why I should keep quiet about it,' she interrupted, fiercely. 'The past is one thing you can do nothing about. I'm sick of trying to push it away from me. I'm sick of pretending. I know it'll always come back and ruin everything!'

Her voice had risen and her eyes had flared, and yet everything appeared to be under control, almost as though these were lines that had been rehearsed. Martin reacted as someone might in an audience, observing the distress and measuring the skill with which it was delivered, but not for a minute thinking that what was being said was wholly real.

'Please,' he said. 'I can see how upset you are. I don't know why. But if there's anything I can do to help – '

'I'm beyond help. I'm out of reach,' she cried, in a style that went out of fashion long before she was born.

Martin rushed across to her, propelled by the same antique melodrama, and almost before he knew what he was doing, knelt beside her chair and took hold of her already clasped hands.

'Oh, my dear,' he said. 'Oh, you poor little thing.'

He realized at the same time that his left knee was hurting, because he had gone down too quickly.

Helen allowed his hands to enfold hers for long enough to accept the concern, and then pulled away. It passes the time, she thought. It helps the day go by. She even managed to notice that the skin on his hands was much rougher than one would have supposed. Estate agents were alleged to be smooth all over.

In his new position, on his knees beside her chair, Martin's head was at such an angle, and at such proximity, that he was able to see almost all of her right breast. He had an over-whelming urge to reach across and slide his hand into her unbuttoned blouse, and forgot about the previously disconcerting twinge in his bent knee.

'You wouldn't say that if you knew the truth,' she said. 'You wouldn't think I was a poor little thing at all. I've brought it all on myself, Martin. It's my own fault.'

'No, no,' he moaned, meaninglessly, and let his hand do what he was wanting it to do. Any risk seemed worth it as he brushed against and then enclosed the swell of her flesh.

'I haven't always been Helen – ' she started to say, appearing not to notice what he was doing.

'Helen. Oh, Helen,' he interrupted, with a soft moan, at the same time shifting on his knees to get into a more comfortable position.

'I used to go under another name. I called myself something else. I did things you would never dream I had done – '

But he was scarcely listening. 'Mmm. Yes. Mmm,' he said, as though in sympathetic agreement, but searching for her mouth with his.

'Martin. Please listen to me, and then you will understand – '

The last syllable was not completed. His tongue had suddenly pushed between her lips. She tried to pull back, but without sufficient conviction to discourage him. He mewed and sucked and licked at her mouth, as sexually excited as he had ever been.

Even if he had heard the crunch of another car on the

gravel around the house, he would not have been able to stop. She was arching her back as he half pulled himself up to get his body next to her. The chair was big enough for both of them. You only get so many chances in this life, he thought, as he pawed at her clothes, and the thing is to take them when you can.

24

John lay still in the bed in the half-darkness, no longer listening to the unlovely sounds of the sleepers around him, nor concerned any more about attracting the attention of the nursing auxiliary dozing at the table at the far end of the ward. He knew now that he had been put in this place because he had lost his memory. It was unlikely that they had yet tracked down his identity, unless he had said something to them which gave them sufficient clues.

He had no idea what had gone on during the time of his loss, but he could now remember everything which led up to it. And how he wished that he did not! It was no wonder that his mind had sought oblivion, and it would have been better if he could have stayed in the mysterious world they had found him in. Whatever phantoms may have leered and gibbered at him in the time that had disappeared could not have been as bad as the ones he had already seen.

An unexpected tinkling and trickling sound made him turn his head. He thought, instantly, of an issue of blood, and his throat was ready to let go of the yelp of fear it had kept at the ready.

A dark shape stood in the space between his bed and the next one. John bit off his cry just in time. He saw, dimly, that it was a man urinating into a bottle. A thin fellow with a head too big in proportion to the rest of his body. He was making small grunting sounds of satisfaction.

John wondered why his neighbour was using a urine bottle when he was obviously capable of getting out of bed, and therefore, presumably, of going to wherever the lavatories were.

'Piss-piss-piss-piss,' the man hissed softly between his teeth like a cat owner with an odd accent calling in his pet.

And then he seemed to stiffen, and he turned to look at John, shaking off the last few drops into the bottle, and pulling down on his penis as though it were made of elastic.

'What?' he said, aggressively. 'What? What?'

John was too startled to reply, but the man shuffled right up to the side of the bed, clutching the almost full bottle threateningly.

'What?' he said again, his eyes bulging in a large and bony skull.

'I didn't say a thing. Not a word,' John said, quickly.

The man clutched with his free hand and took hold of John's hair before the evasive jerk away could be completed.

'What you doing – ' he gasped as the man tugged too hard.

'Scalp ya focking scalp ya,' the man said in a low voice. 'Pissing is private! Engages privates!'

'Nurse! Help! Nurse!' John cried, as his attacker all but lifted him bodily by the hair.

Suddenly, the man let go. He grinned at John in the darkness, showing a broken row of teeth, and without another word shuffled back to his own bed, his large head sunk down into his shoulders. The urine bottle went clunk on the tiled floor, but stayed upright and unbroken.

The nurse had not responded to John's frightened call. Her head was now on her arms, and she was deeply asleep. All around the ward, sighs and grunts, and bubbly snores showed that no one had been disturbed. It might never have happened.

John began to tremble under the bedclothes, for he had pulled the sheet up as high as his eyes as soon as his attacker had left.

This is a psychiatric ward, he thought. The instant these words came into his mind, the trembling stopped.

Cautiously, he lowered the sheet and squinted across at the neighbouring bed. The man was a hump. He was already asleep again.

They are mad in here. They are all out of their minds.

But, of course, now that he thought about it, they might have good reason for assuming that he was the same. God only knows what he had said and done during the period of his 'absence', so to speak. How long had it been? A day? A week? Perhaps a month. There was no measure he could use.

What have I come to? How will I survive?

He let a flutter of questions subside, for they had been sent up like a flock of startled pigeons. In a while, he was able to order his thoughts again. A hint of steely light at the far window showed that morning was on its way, so he had to have a plan ready. The hustle and bustle which always accompanied the start of the day in any institution would provide the best chance of escape. His one advantage was that he now knew who and what he was, but they didn't.

In the nature of things, however, they would eventually discover his identity. He would be arrested, and put away, perhaps until he was a useless and spiritless old man, unable to fend for himself in the novelties and horrors of the future world.

The trembling began again. He had to tighten his jaws.

Where were his clothes, and his money? How could he find them? Where was this hospital? What day of the week was it?

Had they found the body yet?

The trembling stopped, but his skin felt colder as he corrected himself. Bodies. Had they found the bodies yet?

25

'No, no,' she said, as her skirt rode up to her thighs.

'Yes,' Martin gasped. 'Oh, yes. Yes. I must! Please, please, please!'

Helen twisted her mouth away from his wet and foraging lips, but her body was still arched to meet his. He had heaved himself up into the chair, so that his knees were on either side of her. His hands were as busy as his mouth. One set of scrabbling fingers had released his trouser zip, and the other had pulled up her skirt and hooked into the top of her panties. He intended to waste no time. His eyes were bits of blackness, and he was already out of breath. Way back in the past he had rehearsed such a scene as this, as an adolescent desperately masturbating.

Martin slid his mouth downwards from her apparently protesting mouth towards her already mostly exposed breasts. The pinkish glow of her nipple so exhilarating him that he was completely unaware of the stiffness of her right arm as it groped away from the chair. Her hand was pushing aside the bowl of fruit on the small table beside them, disturbing a tiny fly which had long since settled on the ripe spot of a speckled pear.

'Oh, you little devil,' she said. 'You dirty devil.'

He liked that. Indeed, he wished she would use stronger language. The idea of his friend's wife, a well-spoken, middle-class young woman, fouling her mouth with gutter phrases would have had an especial charm as he plunged into her.

'I am, I am!' he gasped, somehow manoeuvring himself

into her, but almost collapsing further down on to her as he made his first, compulsive thrust. 'Oh, you bitch. You dirty bitch. Say you are. Say you are!'

Helen laughed and lifted herself up for him. Her groping hand had found what she wanted, and it was not only to humour him that she shouted out what he had invited her to say. 'I'm a dirty bitch!' she cried. 'I'm a whore!'

The language she was using with such abandon, and the novelty of the position, threatened to cause for him a premature ejaculation. He made a conscious effort to slow the urgency of his drive into her, but after she had shouted so obscenely she began to moan and twist her head, commanding him not to stop and not to slow down. There was nothing more he could do but obey.

In a little more than another minute, he was ready to come. His hands gripped harder on her swivelled hips, and he threw his head back, almost as though it were as much a pain as a triumph, or a closing-in instead of a release.

'Yes!' he said, and 'Yes!' she said, as they rocked together, and then the pain that was coiled under his physical joy was suddenly much worse. The wet spurting at his loins was duplicated in his stomach, and the cry in his mouth rapidly fell down into a gurgle in his throat. He was lurching backwards out of the chair, his eyes at first glassy and then wide with shock. The blood pumped out of him more forcefully than the semen had done, quickly covering that part of the blade of the knife which was not buried in him.

Martin sprawled on the carpet, his hands going to the wound, his eyes raking the white ceiling as though some explanation might be written there.

'Dad,' he said, inexplicably, 'Daddy,' and then nothing more.

Helen waited. 'Who's your father?' she said, eventually. There was no answer, and his face was already the colour of old tobacco ash. She giggled, and fell silent, still in the chair, her skirt still reeved up, her panties down, and small milky globules on her pubic hair.

She stood up, and adjusted her clothing.

'Whatever else you may care to give me,' she said to the bleeding corpse on the living-room floor, 'is a personal transaction between you and me.'

She sat down again, as untroubled as at any time since she had awakened that day, and reviewed the matter, and once again considered what she had long since insisted upon to herself to be her own history. A biography collected out of a brief period of indifferent promiscuity in the long summer holiday immediately after she had left school, the wretched relationship between her parents, a spate of newspaper stories about someone called the Maltese Falcon, and her husband's intermittent, shy, more than half-ashamed, and yet demanding sexual fantasies.

The story which she was telling to herself, as steadily as any of the instalments of 'A Book at Bedtime' on Radio 4 each evening, had reached the stage where the unexpected punter – the white knight – had turned upon the sniggerers at the next table. The piano was tinkling, the park was dark green through the window, and he had hardened his face, looked at them, looked at all the men in the world, and said: 'Is there anything you want?'

'Sorry?' said one of them. The teeth-clicker, the pincher, the leerer, the winker, shover, nudger, look-down-your-front, toucher and innuendo-sprayer. The oaf. The wallowing pig.

'You seem to be more interested in what is going on over here than in your own affairs,' John had said. 'Would you like to sit with us?'

She had played many times with this scene. Sometimes the piano player was in the middle of 'Who's Sorry Now?' and occasionally he had started the first few bars of 'I'm Getting Sentimental Over You'. The faces of the men at the next table were similarly capable of change. Her father was seldom there, but many of the men who had come to his house when she was an adolescent put their faces on those hunched and embarrassed shoulders. But whatever else changed, the words stayed the same. The words and his sweet, sweet face.

And now he had gone and left her.

'Which is,' she said out loud, looking down at the body, 'no more than I deserve. I am an embarrassment to him.'

She laughed once more, but not at the disparity between what she had said and what she had done. It was more in relief than anything else, and the sound of it gave her the energy to get up out of the soft chair again and take hold of Martin's ankles. There was a long way to pull him, over the carpet, out into the tiled hall, and all the way up the stairs, past the turn, and across the landing to the bedroom. It would have been much easier to have asked him upstairs in the first place.

26

In his head, John half heard his old, secret friend call behind him as he left his seat to go to the dining car. 'Think about what you want! Look after yourself!' He let the voice stay, and walked on without it. 'Think about what I want?' he thought. 'That's the trouble. That's all I ever do.'

In a tired and chastened mood, he ordered and ate his food without relish, scarcely looking at his plate and taking no notice of the changing views through the window. His initial pleasure about being on a cross-country train again had been lost in the anxieties of his internal supervision.

Gradually, he slowed his jaws and ceased to swallow. I am being overwhelmed, he thought. The blight is upon me.

And still, among it all, snatches of lovely oblivion, and snatches of renewal – odd, wintry flowers upon the withered stem, yet new, strange flowers such as my life has not brought forth before, new blossoms of me.

John knew that he had been 'let go' by the advertising agency because of his increasing moodiness and introspection. Supposedly overseeing the art work for a new series of advertisements which used the mostly unclothed female body to give new life to the badly flagging market for personal computers, John had day after day found that first the photographs and then the drawings merged or tangled into his own fantasies. He was appalled.

When he came home for his long weekends, and when Helen came up to the ramshackle little mews house near Paddington station, some of the distortions brought up by his working life reached into the ways he talked and dealt with her.

For a long time past, John had been fascinated and repelled by the idea of prostitution and the sight of prostitutes. There was a girl he could see through the tiny window of the Paddington house, who regularly patrolled the wider street off the mews. It was on her turn to retrace her slow patrol that he was able to catch sight of her. She had long black hair, small white boots, long legs and a slender figure.

'Look! There she is! Look at her,' he had said to Helen, making her stand with him at the small window at the top of the metal spiral of a stair. And Helen had looked sidelong at him, puzzled and potentially offended by the strange tightness in his voice.

'Imagine what it would be like for a man to – ' he broke off as he took in her look.

'What do you mean? John?'

'No. I'm sorry. It doesn't matter,' and he stared out of the window again, a flush rising to his cheekbones.

'No. Tell me. Imagine what?'

'Oh, really, Helen. You are so naïve. And you are so prudish – '

'Prudish? Am I prudish?'

What a ridiculous thing for him to say. She was of the generation which regarded any accusation of any variant of puritanism as being patronizing and probably downright insulting. He had not answered her incredulous questions, so, for once, she went over to the attack.

'You're the one to talk,' she said. 'You don't enjoy making love, even when you say you do. Look at the way you turn your head after you've – after we've done it. Do you know how silent you become, for minutes at a time?'

He had certainly gone silent then. His eyes were still fixed on the now empty street corner, but he was not really looking out of the window, and the flush had not left his face.

Helen always worried if she offended him, or thought she

had. Their few disagreements had almost always ended in her quick retreat, even when he was the one admitting error. She reached for his hand, but his fingers stayed limp, refusing to curl around hers.

'She looks attractive,' she said, in a different voice. 'I mean, for what she is. From this distance.' Poor Helen. Oh, poor Helen!

John remembered how he had not answered, and how he had not moved his face. It must have shown her how disturbed he had been. She squeezed his hand, and said his name, questioningly. Only then did he turn his face and speak to her, and he recalled now, on the train, precisely what he had said.

'You're absolutely right. I don't enjoy it. I *do* turn my head away when I've finished, and, yes, I *am* quiet afterwards. I'm chewing on what feels to me like anguish or an extreme disappointment. But do you think that has nothing to do with you? Do you believe you have no responsibility for this, for the way I feel? For the way I find myself looking at that girl out there, or looking at other girls I see during the day, and wondering about them? Do you?'

John stared out of the train window, abandoning his meal.

There was no question but that it was a terrible thing for a husband to say to his wife.

'You're absolutely right.' And then each word like a nail driven into her heart. 'I don't enjoy it. I *do* turn my head away when I've finished, and yes, I *am* quiet afterwards. I'm chewing on what feels to me like anguish or an extreme disappointment.'

We never know, he thought, we never know how cruel we can be, nor guess at the moment when we show it.

Damp fields were sliding by, indifferent to his guilt, and a distant horse cropping grass did not bother to lift its head to look at the noisy express. A single dead elm sent back the only acknowledgement.

Helen had pulled away from him with a small sound in her throat, and then had stared at him with round eyes. If she had been a tougher person, strong inside, with a full hold on her own sense of herself, his words would not have been so dangerous.

He knew that she was a fantasist, and had often enjoyed that in her. In conventional terms, she had been called 'a neurotic' by those who had shared some part of her teenage life. Her mother, more brutally, had simply called her mad.

John asked for his bill, unable to take any more of the sight or the smell of food. He was in any case anxious about his portfolio, unattended as it was back in the carriage. Those paintings held the hope of his future regeneration, and of hers too. They had been made out of his skill, his shame, his dedication and his self-discipline. How foolish of him to place them in the slightest risk.

Exhaustion drooped itself on his shoulders as he moved back along the swaying train to his seat, occasionally bumping his hip against the sides of the supports. He felt as though he were drunk.

That is the trouble, he thought. I have overdone it. I've drained myself, and found too many things in the swamp at the bottom.

Including the Presence he had, as a child, thought of as his secret friend. He was surely the one who was causing all the damage and distress. The most important thing to do therefore was to sit down and think as hard as he could about the best way of destroying him once and for all.

27

Helen was half-way up the stairs when the telephone began to ring. She did not know for the moment whether it was better to go on up and answer it in her bedroom, or run back down to the hall and take it there. The indecision seemed to be of little consequence, and yet such was her mood that she believed that the wrong choice would somehow prove to be catastrophic.

As she freed her limbs from their hesitation, the thought was also released in her that the distance between imagination and responsibility is perhaps as short as the choice she had just encountered. A few clattering steps. A turn one way or the other.

'Hello?' she said, a little out of breath, and hoping with all her strength that it was her husband. She caught sight of herself in the mirror near the telephone as she spoke, and noticed that one too many of the little pearl buttons of her blouse was undone.

28

The young man in the publishing house had not been anything like as enthusiastic as Helen's imagined lines for him.
He had readily agreed that the wild-flower illustrations were
of fine quality, and that the colours were strikingly authentic.
But John had to push away the thought that these compli-
ments had been delivered in much the same way a man
might throw a coin into a good pavement artist's hat.

'I don't want to discourage you, of course,' he said, with
the weak smile which might have been especially rehearsed
for such a phrase.

He was bending over the lovingly detailed picture of the
deeply divided leaves and the yellow daisy head of Oxford
ragwort.

'Thank you,' John said, as calmly as he could manage.

'Very fine,' mumbled the publisher, suddenly embarrassed.
'Very-very. Indeed. I like the glint of – yes, that *is* a glimpse
of railway line, isn't it? Behind the plant.'

John tasted his own misery, like a spurt of bile.

'Yes. It is,' he said. 'But that is not intended to be a
decoration, you know.'

'I didn't suppose it was.'

Christ, thought John. Christ! Why is it people can never be
told anything?

'The point about the railway line,' he said, steadily, 'is that
Oxford ragwort became widespread in the southern part of
England and Wales because of the Great Western Railway. It
is a flower with a fascinating history.'

The young man made a brief humming sound, which

could have been understood as an expression of interest. John was just as English, and knew that, on the contrary, the sound was actually close kin to a yawn. But he could not have been more wrong.

'Originally,' he said, emphasizing the syllables in a way that showed he clearly intended to be a bore, as punishment or revenge, 'it grew in the botanic garden at Oxford. An introduced plant, you see. But then it escaped, and began to grow on some of the old walls which are of course to be found in abundance in that city.'

'Yes, yes,' nodded the publisher, his lips against his teeth.

'But the seeds of the ragwort, as you can see from the small side illustration here – they are parachutes, are they not?'

John savoured the intonation of his father's voice, and knew well what the expression on the publisher's face was trying to hide.

'These parachute hairs were to turn out to be extremely useful so far as the spread of the plant was concerned. When the railway opened between Oxford and London in – ah – '

'Eighteen hundred and forty-four,' said the publisher, unexpectedly.

John's own chute suddenly lost its billow of air. 'Yes,' he said in a different voice. 'That's right. Eighteen forty-four.'

'The Great Western was *properly* so called,' the publisher said. 'I think it is probably fair to claim that the GWR was the finest line in Great Britain and, in terms of precedent at least, the entire world.'

The atmosphere in the room had perceptively improved. John saw in the other's eyes the half-crazed dazzle of those grown men (and they are always men) who enthuse about old railway locomotives or postage stamps or seventy-eight rpm gramophone records.

'I don't think that there can be much argument about that,' he said, only a little ashamed of what felt like fawning.

'None at all. None at all.' The publisher clasped his hands

behind his back, bent forward in a curious little bob, and grinned ferociously.

Perhaps we are all off our heads, thought John, perhaps the whole country is quietly and steadily going completely mad. But he did not want to get trapped into a conversation about railway trains. One of them would end up going, 'Puff-ha-puff-ha-whooo-ooo!' with a shuffle of feet, and arms used as pistons, all around the office. On the other hand, some discreet ingratiation might shove the bloody locomotive on to a more congenial stretch of the track.

'A parachute of seeds is extremely light. After all, it is nothing more than a ring of fine hairs – ' he began.

The listener's alarming grin fixed, and the eyes lost some of their shine. 'Mmmm mm,' he sort of said.

'And when you consider the rush of a locomotive and its wagons, the turbulence of the air, that is, when a train passes – '

'Whumpf – huff-a-puff,' said the publisher.

'Quite. Well, then, the seeds, too, get thrown up into the air, and some of them alight on the carriages, or on the coal or – anywhere on the train, yes? The ragwort soon found its way on to the grassy embankments. I mean, one of these plants, just one of them, can produce eight, nine, ten thousand seeds.'

'Imagine,' said the publisher, his thoughts elsewhere.

Both men became silent and each looked speculatively at the other.

'These are very fine paintings. No question. It's just that – '

'I have been especially concerned with accuracy, both of scale and of colour, as well as particular detail, of course.'

'A labour of love. Yes. Indeed, yes. That is immediately evident.'

'The flora of the railway embankment,' John said, attempting to place another dab of bait, 'provides us with many fascinating examples of the way in which weeds and wild flowers make their way in the world. Some people have made a study of what is happening in the strips of land which lie between the motorways – well, the same sort of thing happened in the last century, with the railway expansion. My text, of course, points this out where necessary.'

The publisher had his hand up to his chin before John finished what in his old job he would have been forced to call 'a creative pitch'.

'Of course, at the end of the day, I'm afraid,' the man said, with a polite hint of disdain for the less than gentlemanly imperatives of the business, 'we have to consider whether or not a particular ah – volume, *book* that is to say, is in a sense marketable, as they say.'

John had met these strange patterns of speech many times before in his working life. They were like a dance of lumbering creatures, weaving their way across a foreshore, their sealed and horny backs always to the sea, as though unwilling to acknowledge its vastness and its perpetual roar.

'I'm very good at trains, too,' he said. 'I enjoy painting locomotives as well.'

'Steam, you mean?' The question was a wolfish pounce.

'Oh, yes! Of course.' John let out a sigh. 'Steam, yes.'

He had not meant to sigh quite so heavily. But it was all right. The fellow took up the same sound and amplified it into the hiss of an expiring engine, and his face was alive with joy.

29

When he finally got back home, not wholly despondent but still very disappointed, John paid off the taxi which had brought him from the station, and turned to look at the house he loved and would not be able to keep. A definite commission to do three full-page plates and four small illustrations for a forthcoming picture book about Great Trains, Great Travels, and the promise to 'review' the possibilities of his wild-flower compendium was better than nothing, but a poor enough reward for his months of diligent toil. The house was a luxury. A smaller one would have to do, even one shoulder to shoulder with its neighbours.

It was almost dusk, and the September sky beyond the long, low, greying hill on the far side of the house looked like a slow river meandering through silt. The air was cool and fresh and mildly perfumed, but this was the time of day that he least liked. Somewhere, a church organ moaned that the day thou gavest, Lord, is ended, and that somewhere was always in wait at the back of his mind.

The light, too, played tricks at this hour, changing distances and outlines, imitating melancholy, teasing at memory, pretending a peace in which opposite things lay hidden. Even so, John wanted to walk along the path and under the dark and now shuddering tree, down to the pond. There were lights on in the house, but the curtains were still open, and another few minutes would not matter. The very way in which the rooms awaited him, light splashing in oblongs against the gloom of the stone, made him want or need to postpone his entry into them.

Without knowing it, and without acknowledging his growing unease, he began to whistle or, rather, hiss out an old nursery rhyme between his teeth as his feet crunched on the gravel. But he stopped the tuppenny rice and the sound of his shoes as soon as he came out from under the darkening spread of the big tree. He had the strangest, and most fleeting of impressions that someone was standing in an attitude of utmost dejection at the edge of the pond, and that someone was himself.

He knew, of course, that this was impossible, and as soon as the mistaken sight had been taken in, it went. There was nobody by the pond. It was an illusion caused, no doubt, by the poor light, the mood of the evening, and his own unrelieved tiredness. Nevertheless, he did not continue on his way to the pond, where the dark of the water met the dark in the sky and sent up a few curling wisps of uncertain greeting. The illusion had been disturbing enough to make him want the lighted rooms, and shapes with distinct edges.

John turned back, and as he moved he heard, behind him now, a plop! from the pond. It was exactly the sound of a pebble being tossed into the water. John did not look back, and the crunch-crunch of his feet on the gravel became faster and louder. He was oddly relieved to reach the front door, especially after he noticed that his own shadow took shape on the path and then the stone of the wall. It must be the porch light, he thought, unwilling to work out that, if it were, the shadow would have shrunk and not grown.

The dim and insubstantial shape appeared to go into the house ahead of him, and then was lost in the welcoming glow of light. Helen was stepping forward to meet him, and his spirits rose at the sight of her, for she looked lovely.

He had determined, at last, how to banish his former secret friend, the other John. And it was not too late: it must not be too late. Then both of them could be free: no, all three of them.

30

Where were his clothes, and his money? How could he find them? Where was this hospital? What day of the week was it?

Had they found the body yet?

The trembling stopped, but his skin felt colder as he corrected himself. Bodies. Had they found the bodies yet?

He fixed his attention on the high window where the light would soon go from slate to silver and reviewed the horror of his homecoming and his subsequent flight.

The dusk held within it the promise of peace, and he was prepared to overcome disappointment in the same diligent manner he had trained himself to bring to his work. The house would have to be sold, but he had already set that process in motion. He was already beginning to feel a stranger in it, and he went down to the pond with the air of a tenant rather than an owner.

Plop! went the water, as he threw in a small stone, and brooded awhile, his thought going outward like the ripples, and fading away into nothingness. How long had he stood there?

Long enough, certainly, to see the reeds on the opposite side merge into the dusk and lose all separateness. Long enough for the lights in the house to splash far out across the grass and the gravel paths. He recalled, now, the way he had turned to look at the windows, vivid shapes in the dark, and the substance of his thoughts as he had done so.

Behind those blazing windows, in one of those rooms, was his enemy, the woman. His 'enemy', he thought, looking at the house, because she would not or could not enter his world with him. She was therefore a judge. One of those who said this was right and that was wrong. Like his father. The way she sometimes looked at him, stared at him, put him in mind of the way the old clergyman had once upon a time examined him over the top of his spectacles. Not then the nod and the hum and click as the teeth were brought together, the signal of his father's disapproval, but from her a cold glitter in the eyes and a reluctance to perform.

To perform, to perform.

Standing by the pond, the evening cool against his skin, he had once more burned inside. The two nights in London had helped for a while to slake his thirst, but expensively so. The Irish girl's thin bracelets had clinked and chinked together as her long fingers moved up and down, slow and then fast and then slow, making him slippery, and then, after another wrangle about money, and then her head coming over, her mouth replacing her fingers, and the fall and quiver of her breasts seen through the angle of her arm. The next one he had found soliciting in Sussex Gardens, and she was still a half-child, even in her corruption, and he had mounted her from behind rather than spoil his pleasures by any glimpse of her bad teeth.

Even now, the bedclothes on him, the grunts and groans in the half-dark around him, he stirred at the loins, thinking of what he had been thinking at the pond in the garden of his home. 'Former home,' he corrected himself.

But I'm not going to live here, and he looked sideways at the crazy man with the big head, *they're not going to keep me in here.*

He had crunched his way back to the house, dark in the dark, and he had the set on his face which she would recognize. Helen would have to discard Helen and take him as Penny, the whore. To perform, to perform: and to bring him some ease, to sell him some peace. *The bitch!*

'The bitch,' he said, out loud. 'The mad bitch.'

Penny had been waiting for him, all right. She licked and nibbled at his face, in the way he had demanded, and she was dressed in the way he wanted, and she had led him up the stairs in the way he had dreamed she might. He had been too excited to notice the blood on the steps, or the taste of sulphur on her tongue, or the deadly jet spots in the centre of each of her eyes.

Hanging in the wardrobe, among the clothes, were Martin and Angela, each of them struck through the middle with a knife.

'And they deserve it,' she said, as she turned on him, the scream rising in absolute hate, higher by far than his own.

He had long considered this to be the true bond between the sexes. The other John was a threatened, modern man, at one with the culture around him. He was not so easily killed.

31

When Helen stepped forward to meet him, his spirits rose at the sight of her, for she looked lovely. But then he noticed that her smile, though determined, was tentative and anxious in a truth impossible for her face to hide. There was a candour to her expression which had often served her ill, and it tugged at him now, making him feel soiled, the giver of pain or the bringer of darkness.

'Hello,' he said.

'Hello,' she said, and her smile was already less tentative.

They stood and looked at each other, mutually shy. He heard the throaty tick-h, tock-h of the inherited clock in the hall, but its measure was, for this moment, without meaning.

'I thought something had gone wrong,' she said, with a small movement of her hands, an echo of nervousness. 'I thought you weren't going to come back.'

'Not come back?' his face opening into incredulity. Had things been so bad, then? Had he really herded such thoughts into her head? Were both of them infected by his sick fantasies?

'When you didn't phone. And then when the phone did go, it was Martin.'

'Martin? Oh, no! Did he – ?'

She nodded. 'He said he thought he had someone who wanted to buy the house and – '

He quickly enclosed her in his arms, almost before her voice broke and the tears came. And then, in the way of these things, he began to weep with her as they rocked together, enfolded.

But the tears, for both of them, were not because of grief. They came because each of them thought that from now on everything was going to be all right.

The snatch of renewal was always and everywhere better than the snatch of oblivion.

'Everything is going to be all right,' he whispered to her, his wet face close to hers. 'You'll see.'

She nodded and laughed and nodded and cried, hugging him all the time, hoping and believing that what he said, and now kept repeating, was true.

'But your work – ?' she asked, in a little while, pulling back in his arms the better to see his face. She had long sensed that if he could only get that right, then –

'Odd, wintry flowers,' he said, and laughed, like a boy's laugh.

Later that night he had tried to explain to her what he had meant, but had been unable to do so. He had telephoned Martin Stoner before they had gone to bed to tell him to hold off the sale of the house in case things changed. Helen could see, could almost touch, the renewal of confidence and optimism in him. He made her laugh with some choo-choo noises, in an exaggerated account of the meeting in London, and told her that he didn't object at all to doing pictures of old locomotives instead of the wild flowers of his father's sermons.

'I am going to be a painter again,' he said. 'A real one.'

Locomotives and tansy, wagons and Oxford ragwort were to be as nothing, mere journeyman exercises. There was far more demanding work to be done.

'Good,' she said, wriggling closer to him, reassured enough now not to listen too keenly.

He could see the stoop of the hedgerow, the cold aloofness of the single dead elm, and a horse cropping grass in a damp field, the sky falling slowly down on to its back. It would make a haunting landscape, an accomplishment beyond anything he had yet even attempted.